T0285376

The Environmental Alarmist

Alarmist

(A Political Satire)

Michael Contarino

The Environmental Alarmist

Alarmist

(A Political Satire)

Addison & Highsmith

Addison & Highsmith Publishers

Las Vegas ◊ Chicago ◊ Palm Beach

Published in the United States of America by
Histria Books
7181 N. Hualapai Way, Ste. 130-86
Las Vegas, NV 89166 USA
HistriaBooks.com

Addison & Highsmith is an imprint of Histria Books. Titles published under the imprints of Histria Books are distributed worldwide.

Library of Congress Control Number: 2023938034

ISBN 978-1-59211-307-1 (hardcover)
ISBN 978-1-59211-319-4 (eBook)

To my parents and grandparents

PART ONE

Man is not what he thinks he is,

he is what he hides.

— André Malraux

They were hungry and moved fast, trampling fields, devouring crops and dropping their waste everywhere. As their numbers swelled, they invaded towns, dug up gardens, parks, backyards and golf courses. News reports of attacks on people and domestic animals advised children to drop their schoolbags and climb a tree if they heard grunting by the roadside.

"We've got to stop this, Marco! I'm the goddamn 'Environmental President!' – the guy who was going to get this under control!" There was a helplessness in his eyes I had not seen before.

Kate stood by the window, watching green flies swarm across the Rose Garden, making ticking sounds as they impacted the glass, like winged lemmings. She turned toward me and raised her arms in frustration. Beads of sweat slid down her sides – the White House was 100% solar, but Hernandez had insisted on setting the air conditioning to 80 F degrees.

I rubbed the back of my neck with both hands as Kate shuffled and stared at me. I had nothing but admiration for the First Lady, but I ignored her silent plea that I keep my mouth shut.

I placed both hands on the President's desk and leaned toward him: "What the hell do you want me to do, Dick? You think another pretty speech will stop thousands of goddamn genetically modified pigs?" My tone was harsher than I intended. Kate winced.

"Mr. President," I tried to speak slower and to soften my voice, but the effort only made me sound annoyed – my words came out staccato, like the flies hitting the window. "Homeland Security will contain the infestation as best they can, sir. Until the sterilization program is ready, or until Congress gets off its ass."

I was about to add that, in the meantime, the pigs were going to keep breeding, and there wasn't anything we could do about it. But Kate's glare induced me to stop talking.

"What about hunters?" he insisted. "Any word from the NRA?"

How ironic. Dick Hernandez, the most liberal President since Roosevelt, was trying to get help from the gun nuts.

"Dick," Kate tried to say it gently, "the only thing those fools care about is making sure you don't get re-elected, and…"

I interrupted her – better that I take the heat – "…and open season laws won't make the pigs any better to eat. Seems the gen-mod produced some kind of protein that makes people sick. Hunters aren't going to help us, Mr. President. We've done what we can until Congress votes."

That wasn't what he wanted to hear, but it was true. Post-Crisis reforms required that Congress authorize most National Guard mobilizations, and the Republicans were dragging their feet, trying not to look too gleeful as Dick's approval numbers sank.

As the politicians dallied, farmers and ranchers took matters into their own hands, organizing militias to protect their crops. But these "pig patrols" had attracted common criminals and conspiracy theorists claiming that the swine were a government plot. Some had the nasty habit of shooting at anything that moved, including dogs, cats, and homeless people sleeping in the woods.

As the smell of rotting animal carcasses wafted through communities, the CDC reported the re-appearance of infectious diseases eliminated decades before. And, to ice the cake, the Canadians sent troops to the border for the first time since a 19th century territorial dispute between the US and the British Empire.

The irony was lost on no one that the 1859 conflict had been called the "Pig War."

Dick's voice cracked as he looked at me with moist eyes:

"Marco, the optics are terrible. Let's do a speech demanding Congress fund a pig-eradication drone force. Or, something?"

I stood away from the desk and placed both hands on my lower back, pushing thumbs into sore muscles. I bent backward and looked toward the ceiling as I spoke:

"Mr. President. This isn't about optics. It's about pigs. Tens of thousands of nasty, mean-ass, genetically modified pigs who eat everything in sight, who shit everywhere, and who fuck like bunnies. Another speech won't change that. Sir."

As I turned back toward him, I observed the flies slamming against the window. The green ooze they left on the pane descended slowly, reminding me, for some reason, of that terrible moment years ago when Mary had warned me that opportunity knocks but once.

"It's too late, sir." I stared into his eyes. "Too late for speeches. No more clever words, Dick. No more political bullshit."

He sighed and was about to say something. I straightened and placed my hands on his desk again. I leaned in.

"So you can go to hell. Sir."

Chapter One

You ask me how it began? It began two years earlier under very different circumstances. In another world, really. Let me take you there - to that sheltered world I inhabited – before I became a bigshot, before the Pig-gate scandal exploded, before I got subpoenaed by Congress to testify against my dearest friends.

I was sitting there, squirming on a wooden chair, waiting for my turn at the podium. The seat felt rough, the legs uneven, and my thighs bounced under the table, causing the chair to rock. I took a deep breath through my nose, as they had taught me in that stress-management class. I observed the air entering my nostrils – the conference room smelled vaguely like disinfectant and dirty socks. My crotch itched but I couldn't scratch because I was seated next to the speaker, in full view of everyone.

I gazed at Mary at the podium, and nodded knowingly so that I might appear interested in what she was saying. I imagined her as a super-hero whose power was an unnatural ability to bore people to death.

How I hated academic conferences! In a moment, I was supposed to stand up and present my latest silly, borderline-fraudulent research paper – as soon as Mary finished giving her paper on "The Epistemology of Fake News," or whatever the hell it was.

I turned my gaze back to the audience and looked around the room at all the usual suspects – regulars at the annual "Propaganda Studies" panel. In the second row was Omar from New York University, an expert on Artificial Intelligence and Deep Fakes. As at past conferences, Omar had read his paper nervously, never looking up or at the audience. He was a nice enough guy, but talking with him always made me feel uncomfortable, as he stared at the floor or at my teeth. I noticed his hairline had receded another quarter inch or so since last year.

Next to Omar was Ada from the University of New Mexico. Ada had made her name years before with a widely cited article in *Political Psychology* entitled "White Nationalist Rhetoric and the Erotic Black Female Image." I liked Ada, and I had slept with her once, at a conference in Albuquerque several years ago when she was single, and both of us were drunk. I remembered little from that encounter – a few hushed gasps and her immoderate perfume – oh, and that ridiculous pit bull terrier of hers that growled menacingly at me from the foot of the bed, after we tired of it scratching at the door and let it in.

The previous evening at the conference dinner, Ada had gone on about how her new husband was a Native American shaman or something in Santa Fe, and that she had just finished writing a book on whatever-it-was, that I think she said was going to be published by someone-or-other. She raised her hand to ask a question, but I didn't hear it because I was distracted by Sylvia behind her, sitting alone and looking miserable.

Rumor had it that Sylvia was about to lose her job at Syracuse. I didn't know the details, but I felt terrible about it – she and I had been such pals years ago in graduate school, before we got teaching jobs and lost touch. Back then she was always smiling and joking and drinking beer and doing the funniest impressions of our professors. She was a lesbian, which was great, because it meant our friendship never got complicated by the sex thing. She was forever ready for a dare, like that time we went to a party together completely naked with running suits painted on our bodies. How things had changed. Sylvia sat awkwardly, bent forward in her seat. I tried to catch her gaze, but her dark eyes darted from side to side, never meeting mine, looking for the rabid hyena she seemed to fear might lurch from behind a lampshade at any moment.

Behind Sylvia sat several older pedants, male and female, whom I had met at past conferences, but whose names I could never remember. One guy, a caricature of his academic self, right down to the salt-and-pepper goatee and the ratty tweed jacket, leaned forward toward Mary, apparently unaware that his finger was buried knuckle-deep into his left nostril. Some of the old-timers' sagging gray faces, even Professor Finger-Up-My-Nose's, weren't too unpleasant, but others were scowling, and a few appeared downright mean. Angry. Dyspeptic. The way people become when life isn't fun anymore, but they're too afraid or too lazy to do anything about it.

And, of course, there were all the eager youngsters in the front row – bubbly graduate students hoping to join our donnish mutual-admiration society. They gazed at Mary as she droned on in her whiney voice:

"Earlier scholarship focused on rhetorical meaning" – she dragged the word out, so it became "meeEEEning." "But recent theoretical work shows the importance of understanding first what we meeEEEn by 'meeEEEning'...." She obviously thought this was a clever point, because she let out one of her irritating squeaks at the end.

What the hell was she talking about? My stomach clenched, and I sucked again at the fusty air in a futile effort to make the discomfort go away. My crotch still itched, and my legs now were bouncing uncontrollably, as if they belonged to someone else.

It was Mary who finally pushed me over the edge. As she spoke, my gaze drifted to the other side of the room. Light was coming in the window. I heard children playing softball. One of them hit the ball and teammates shouted with delight and cheered as the batter raced around the bases. I remembered playing soccer at school and fishing in a creek with my friend Andrew. I thought of the time I raced my mother across a covered bridge in Vermont when I was seven or eight and the maples were turning red. Mary's voice faded until it was just a rusty door hinge scraping and squeaking as it swung back and forth.

Back and forth. Back and forth.

Something snapped. In a moment of clarity that was also oddly free of thought – I stood up. Something had changed. Maybe everything. I had fantasized about this for years, and now I actually was doing it. Instead of stepping to the podium, praising the previous speaker for her rare insights into whatever-the-hell-it-was, instead of making some clever academic in-joke and then pretending for twenty minutes like I gave a rat's ass about "Normative Consequences of Micro-targeted

Propaganda after the Crisis," I strode past the podium and toward the door. It felt right. It felt good.

Mary fell silent as I passed before her, and all heads turned toward me, but I made no eye contact as I moved toward the exit. They must have thought I was sick. But for the first time in years, I felt truly well. Energized. The sadness that had weighed upon me for so long lifted as I pressed forward. I swung open the door, took a long, deep breath, and gazed forward into the hotel's breezeway.

I still don't completely understand why, but Mary's squeaking had given me the courage to change. To change it all. And as I think I just said, it felt amazing. As I left everything I knew, and the career I had built over so many years, I somehow felt not like I was leaving, but like I was coming home. Coming home from a long, exhausting and fruitless trip.

***

Nearly two decades before, I had decided to get a Ph.D. in political science. I wanted to understand how propaganda worked, so I could teach people how to recognize it. How not to be fooled by it. It was how I was going to make the world a better place. Or at least that's what I told myself. But I should be honest. Maybe I went to grad school only to avoid having to get a job, or otherwise risk doing anything genuine? Harvard offered me a full scholarship -- and the academic career that followed had allowed me to keep the real world at a safe distance for 19 years.

I had been a pretty good graduate student. I wrote a passable dissertation, got a teaching job on a leafy campus near Boston, published several academic articles and one half-decent book *(The Art and Science of Mass Deception: Propaganda in Cultural Context)*. I got tenured, meaning that to lose my job I would have to strangle my department Chair (an unlikely, though not an entirely unthinkable possibility). I sat on college committees and went to conferences and gave a few papers every year. The students loved my classes, and the editors of the student paper even invited me to write a weekly column: "Phake News?"

I was a solid member of the college and the political science department. Most people liked me, and no one suspected what I alone knew: that beneath my earnest exterior there lurked a shameless bullshit artist. My scholarly writing was highbrow doubletalk, and my classes were cheap entertainment for *hoi polloi*. If you ask me – and I know you didn't, but I'm going to tell you anyway – most of my students were grade-grubbing opportunists, un-burdened by anything that might be mistaken for intellectual integrity.

OK. That wasn't fair. It wasn't their fault. It was mine. I was the phony. I was the liar. I was Mr. Phake News, not them. Most were good kids. Sincere and innocent; still relatively uncorrupted by the poses and put-ons and soul-crushing compromises of life. And for a time, I loved working with them – nothing gave me more joy than the look of sudden comprehension in a bright student's eyes. In the early years, I had showered them with tough love, demanding sound arguments based on facts and logic. And showing them how to do it. I really was going to change the world.

But over time, I don't know why, something changed. Maybe I got lazy, or just tired. I stopped challenging them. Instead of trying to educate my students, I settled for getting them to like me – which wasn't hard to do, of course, for Mr. Phake News, the propaganda expert. I told them what they wanted to hear, whether or not it was true. I flattered their prejudices and fed their self-serving delusions. I stoked their egos like a winter fire, and they rewarded my pedagogical cowardice with praise and popularity. That I could become an admired teacher by doing a crappy job was proof, I came to believe, that if there was a God, the Holiest of Holy was a con-artist too.

I got tenured, of course. Strange, isn't it? You lose your ideals and integrity, and they start bestowing honors upon you. I spent my first sabbatical semester as a Visiting Fellow at Oxford, finishing my book – whenever doing so did not interfere unreasonably with my exhaustive study of Oxford's many fine pubs. Then, upon my return to the USA the next Fall, I won several awards, including "Teacher of the Year." Now, these awards are horseshit of course, but I was sad that my mother wasn't still around. She would have been proud of her only child. But at least my friends from The Independent Pub were there to appreciate it – they even made me a framed mock certificate that said "Marco Vannicelli: Teacher of the

Fucking Year!" I hung it behind my desk, where every student could see it, much to my Chair's consternation.

It was about then that I started getting the back pain and the strange, recurrent dream about the little girl in the floral dress. She was running through a crowded outdoor market, somewhere in Italy, crying, looking for her mother. I called out for her to stop. I knew where her mother was. I wanted to help her, but I was out of breath, and she couldn't hear me above the shouts of the fishmongers. She ran faster and faster away. I had forgotten her name.

***

So, there I was, 41 years old, a respected scholar, a popular teacher, an expert in my field. I was cruising down the highway of academic life, when I suddenly decided to take the next exit – without a clue as to where it might lead.

Standing in the doorway, I looked back at Mary and had a bizarre vision. I imagined her stepping away from the podium as she spoke, waddling up to each person in the room, pulling up her skirt, sitting astride their chests and, snorting contentedly, swinging her head from side to side and grinning as she waterboarded them with "meeeEEEning" until, gasping, they begged her to stop.

I recalled when I broke up with her so many years ago, unsure of why I was doing it – and then my years of wondering if I had made a terrible mistake. Mary was brilliant, kind, and trustworthy – my best friend and my safe harbor in the storm of life. My mother loved her like a daughter. It still hurts to remember Ma's face, red and twisted with disappointment when I told her that I was leaving Mary: "*Sei matto, Marco?* Are you crazy?" She had never shouted at me like that. "*Non troverai mai un'altra come lei!* You'll never find another like her!"

But I left Mary, and I hurt terribly the only two people I had ever loved. And I didn't know why! For a while I hated myself. But what, I thought, would life have been with Mary, really? A faculty row Victorian filled with wise-ass, little fake-news Marcos and squeaky little Mary's? College gossip over dinner? Come on – the one real thing I had done in my life was leaving her.

How ironic that now, so many years later, and just as I was finding the courage to change my life – just as I was finally doing something real again after two decades of peddling bullshit – there she was again. Mary, the love of my youth, of all people, was at the podium, giving some ridiculous academic talk on the MeeeEEEning of meaning.

As I looked at her, my knees buckled, but I caught myself by grabbing the doorframe. I scanned the room; everyone was staring at me. They seemed perplexed – except for Mary. Just before I stepped through the door – and I realize I might be wrong about this, but I don't think so – I saw her brown eyes light up and her mouth open into a little smile.

I was in a daze as I left the conference room, so my memory may betray me here, but I'm pretty sure that as I turned back for one last look, a sort of tunnel appeared. It was a tunnel like no other – I was both standing in it, and yet looking at it from the outside. And somehow it went both forward to the future and back to the past. At the far end, the little Italian girl in the floral dress was waving at me.

I grabbed my coat and umbrella, ran down the hall and flew out onto the street, laughing. On the way, I dropped the conference program and my conference pass on the floor of the hotel lobby. The sun was poking through the clouds and the sea breeze felt fresh and cool. I was free. I took a deep breath and tossed my umbrella in a trash can.

A few days later, a meeting with the Dean, and it was done. Karol was a kind soul, and she offered me a leave of absence. I told her to spare herself the paperwork.

"Marco, think of your students! Remember last year's graduation?"

I hesitated a moment before gesturing toward the form on her desk. She pleaded with her eyes as she pushed it toward me. I took out my gold pen and stared at it. I looked at the form. I looked back at the pen. My hand shook as I put it to the paper.

A signature, and the world was new. For the first time in 19 years, I didn't know what to do, but I knew that it would be me, not someone pretending to be me, who would do it. If there was a God, that God would guide me. If not, I would live out my existence in an indifferent, uncaring world. But at least it would not be in the fantasy land of academia. Something genuine, something authentic – in that real world I had avoided all my life – awaited me.

I was scared to death. And it felt great.

Chapter Two

For two decades I had pretended to be someone I wasn't. Now I was nobody. I had no spouse, no family, no obligations, no expectations. No job. Not so much as a cat. Or a goldfish, swimming endlessly in circles around a bowl.

Did I care about what might come next? Was I worried about how to pay my bills? Strangely, not at all – I felt only an exhilarating sense of freedom. And, to my surprise, it felt good to be nobody for a change. I wasn't worried about all the attention and admiration I would no longer enjoy – the lecture halls filled with students, their eyes fixed on me as I dispensed my learned wisdom on the methods and mechanisms of deception and propaganda. None of that seemed to matter. After all, what was all that attention good for really, except to massage the ego of an only child used to being the center of attention?

So, despite the objective precariousness of my situation, I felt light and carefree, unconcerned about what I might do next, or about such mundane matters as where I might live or how long my savings would last. And in these circumstances, I did the only thing that made sense – I bought a plane ticket to Rome. Being nobody has its advantages, particularly if you still have somebody's credit card.

I was born in Italy, and Italian was my first language, although I rarely spoke it anymore since my mother died. She had taken me to live in Washington DC when I was a baby, and she got a job working for the Italian embassy. I had hazy memories of a trip back to Italy to visit my grandparents, and of playing with other Italian children in their courtyard. My mother kept a photo of her parents in her bedroom after they had passed, but she never mentioned my father. Whenever I asked about him, she would say nothing, while tilting her head back and lifting her arm up in the international gesture of someone drinking. After she died, I thought briefly about trying to find him. After all, so far as I knew, he was the only living relative I had. But I was deep into writing my dissertation. And, to be honest, I was afraid of whom I might find.

But if I never had much interest in finding my father, I always had nurtured a fondness for Italy. I had promised myself for years that I would go back as soon as I found the time – and now time was the one thing I had plenty of. I knew that when I returned to Boston in a few weeks, everything would be just as it was – everything except for my one plant, a spindly spidery thing, that would have died, making my new, simplified life even simpler.

***

I was sitting alone at a sidewalk trattoria in Rome, not far from Piazza del Popolo, enjoying the summer heat, a glass of cold Frascati, and a delicious *spaghetti alla gricia* -- as good and simple and genuine as my mother's *farfalle alla zucca*. I listened to the hum of overlapping conversations. I smelled basil and tomatoes and freshly baked bread. A young man gesticulated to his friend as they chatted astride their scooters. A well-dressed older woman at the next table scowled as she read *La Repubblica*. The headline – reversed but visible through her Reader – said something about invasive weeds damaging food-crops. Someone else's children were playing under her table; she smiled and put down her device to make funny faces for them.

I felt a pleasant loneliness as I took another sip of wine. I knew no one in Italy anymore, and no one knew me – and the anonymity felt good. My thoughts drifted to the Italian political thinkers Mary and I had studied in graduate school: Mazzini, Beccaria, Gramsci and, of course, Machiavelli, the paradoxical Renaissance humanist and cynic. I also thought of some of Italy's worst politicians – charlatans like Berlusconi and monsters like Mussolini, whose careers were studies in demagogy and deception. Indeed, I first became fascinated by the power of propaganda when watching, as an undergraduate, a 1930s newsreel of Mussolini speaking to an enthralled Fascist crowd. The dictator's words were nonsense, but the emotions they stirred enabled him to hypnotize Italy for two decades.

I looked out on the piazza. There was a balcony above, not unlike the one on Piazza Venezia nearby, where *il Duce* regularly addressed the masses. I imagined Mussolini, big around the middle, balding and arrogant, strutting across the balcony in military dress, hands on his hips, chin in the air, inciting a crowd below with skilful flattery. I thought of his ally, Adolf Hitler, and his massive Nazi rallies. I took another sip. The wine was sweet on the lips, but astringent on the palate.

As I gazed up and back a century at Mussolini strutting on that balcony, a tall, paunchy, middle-aged man walked into my line of sight. A waiter gestured to the table next to mine, and the man turned and approached. He looked familiar. At first I couldn't place him, but then I realized it was Dick Hernandez, the US Senator from California. He wore blue shorts and brown leather sandals. A grey cotton T-shirt stretched unflatteringly over his ample belly. I never had met the Senator, but I always had considered him an admirable public figure. In interviews, he came across as intelligent, knowledgeable and straight-talking – one of those rare politicians who actually seemed to care about policy and know what he was talking about.

Hernandez was physically unprepossessing, and even on the Stream his suits always looked too tight. But what he lacked in looks he made up for with his unpretentiousness and sincerity. He had come from a poor, industrious Mexican immigrant family, and he had worked his way up through community college and UCLA. People liked him because he seemed like a reliable, friendly, guy-next-door with a bit of extra smarts. He was earnest, always polite, and known for his self-deprecating sense of humor. He liked to joke that, as a boy, he never talked back to his father because his Spanish wasn't good enough. Hernandez had the reputation for being a champion of the environment and of the little guy, and for being squeaky-clean honest – a Latino version of Jimmy Stewart in *Mr. Smith Goes to Washington*.

Indeed, a Washington commentator had gotten himself into trouble recently when asked on *Meet the Press* if he thought Hernandez should run for President. The hapless journalist, thinking he was being funny, had called him "Mr. Brown goes to Washington." The commentator hadn't been seen since on the Sunday news shows. But his point, however inelegantly made, was a good one. Hernandez was eminently qualified to be President, but he was too nice a guy, too uncalculating, to make it to the White House. Voters say they want their politicians to be competent and honest and authentic, but they always fall for the sweet lies of con-artists. Hernandez would make a fine Vice President or Secretary of State. But he lacked the cunning to get elected President.

Hernandez was alone. He sat down just inches from me and explored the menu. He looked less fleshy than on the Stream, but his dark skin was mottled, his jowls were bountiful, and his pitch-black hair was slick and too long for a politician. It curled over his collar and around his ears. The slow but deliberate way he moved reminded me, for some reason, of Mary. He eyed the menu hungrily, but he wasn't smiling. He seemed annoyed about something.

As it happened, I knew a lot about Hernandez, because I had used him as a case study in my freshman class on Political Propaganda. One of the themes of my course was that propaganda works because the politicians and their consultants and media cronies are pros, and the voters are amateurs. Citizens need to know the techniques of the propagandist if they wish to distinguish truth from trickery. I had taught my students that Hernandez was the exception that proved the rule – a sincere, truth-telling, anti-politician. He had risen to the Senate through honest hard work, rather than through rhetoric and showmanship. I told them that Hernandez' successful political career proved that sincere people can sometimes win elections, because people sensed their authenticity.

And now there he was, Latino Jimmy Stewart himself, seated next to me, alone, trying to decide what to have for lunch in a small Roman trattoria. He was probably there for the same reason I was – to get away from his life and to have a moment to himself. Except of course that, unlike me, he still had a life to return to. I knew that his wife, Catherine Richards Hernandez, was a law professor at Georgetown, and a minor celebrity herself because of the cases she had argued before the Supreme Court. He had an adult daughter, Alexandra, and a safe Democratic seat in the US Senate. He had been rising through the ranks in Congress when President Cranmore tapped him to head the Environmental Protection Agency – where he had distinguished himself as a tough leader willing to stand up to the fossil fuels industry. After less than two years at the EPA, he resigned to run for the Senate as an outspoken environmentalist. One of the nation's most well-known Latino politicians, and popular in his home state, Hernandez may not have been presidential material, but he surely was a player on the Democrats' A-team.

I was about to introduce myself when his phone rang. He looked at it coldly as it rang four or five times.

"Yeah what?" His tone was rough.

The caller began, but Hernandez interrupted: "Sit on my face, asshole!"

The woman at the next table turned, and then quickly looked away. He lowered his voice but didn't change his tone: "You could have stayed the hell out of it!"

The caller seemed to be trying to explain, but he interrupted again: "You know what? Fuck you! And anyone who looks like you! And fuck that shithead Obama too!"

Hernandez hung up and grumbled something angrily in Spanish under his breath. Then he smiled. His hands were shaking, but he looked pleased with himself. He turned on the waiter who had arrived at his table, demanding a San Pellegrino and a bottle of Fontana Candida – rudely, but in pretty good Italian.

I was stunned. Not by his bad manners or his vulgarity. Not even because he spoke Italian, although that certainly was unexpected. I was stunned because of how wrong I had been – and I wasn't used to being wrong, especially about politicians.

The Mr. Smith thing, it would seem, was less of an obstacle than I had thought to this guy becoming President of the United States.

Chapter Three

I forced my gaze down to the spaghetti on my plate as I listened to Hernandez and the waiter discuss items on the menu. His voice was calm now, as they bantered about the relative merits of Frascati and Grechetto when paired with different kinds of fish. I thought about what I was hearing and what I had just heard. Mr. Polite, Respectful Nice Guy actually has a hot temper and a foul mouth. The unpretentious, salt-of-the-earth, meat-and-potatoes regular guy, who claimed he was no good with languages, was discussing local wines and Roman recipes with the waiter. In Italian.

I thought back to the lecture on "Image" I used to give in my Political Propaganda course:

"In electoral politics, image is reality. People don't vote for politicians – they vote for the person they imagine a politician to be. Or more precisely, who the politician convinces them he or she is. Campaigns are about constructing a positive image for yourself, and a negative one for your opponent. It's the candidate who does this best that wins the voters' trust. This, of course, has very little to do with actually being trustworthy. Machiavelli put it this way in *The Prince*:

'…men are so simple, and so subject to present necessities, that he who seeks to deceive will always find someone who will allow himself to be deceived…'"

I would then pause, smile, and continue:

"But maybe Groucho said it even better: 'Authenticity: If you can fake that, you've got it made!'"

This always led to some tittering, but I would continue my lecture:

"The research shows that even voters who think they are politically well informed are easily deceived. Even knowledgeable voters are no match for the teams of pollsters, strategists, psychologists, marketers, AI techies, hackers and microtargetters that donor cash pays for. The sad reality is that elections often come down to which team of professionals bamboozles the voters best."

At this point, jaws would drop. Some students would shift in their seats, while others would fold their arms defiantly. Being told you have been fooled, that you aren't as smart as you thought you were, is never easy. But I wasn't there to make it easy. I was there to open eyes. To change the world.

I would continue: "Some campaigns succeed by relentlessly attacking their rivals with negative ads and fake news. But most successful candidates also get voters to trust them by tapping into cultural myths, narratives and archetypes. Reagan was John Wayne, the tough cowboy with a good heart, riding his horse into town to save us from the bad guys. Bill Clinton was the empathetic neighbor who understood what we were going through and felt our pain. George W. Bush, in reality a pampered child of old New England money, presented himself as a plain-talkin', brush-cuttin' Texan. Obama was a Christ figure, the savior promising hope and change. Trump, a conman's conman, convinced millions that he 'told it like it was.' Biden was our reassuring uncle, the trustworthy friend who promised to lead us out of the chaos and division of the early Crisis years. And President Cranmore? Ah, yes. Well, she's our steadfast, reliable aunt, kissing our boo-boos and telling us everything is going to be all right now, and that Mommy and Daddy will be home soon. Meanwhile, the nostalgist Jack Canterbury is Ulysses, looking wistfully toward a lost home, as he prepares to challenge Cranmore, with his yearning call to a mythical, pre-Crisis, 'Real America.'"

Typically, at this point I would try to make eye contact, knowing that this would elicit knowing nods around the lecture hall. Every student recognized these crafted presidential images. Now, thanks to me, they could see how feigned, how phony, but also how seductive they were. And the brighter students would grasp how easy it is to be duped by the mirages politicians fabricate. Because, whether we are thirsty or not, the pols are pros, who know how to make us drink from their wells of lies.

"So it's image that people vote for," I would continue. "But if the candidate is too phony, even we dumb voters can see through it. There's always a bit of reality behind the illusion. Bill Clinton could make us feel like he cared because he was emotionally intelligent and a smooth talker – and he used these skills to present himself as the man who understood the problems of ordinary people. George W. Bush and Ronald Reagan really were cowboys at heart, with little patience for the nuanced arguments of intellectuals. Obama saw himself as an agent of change and new hope, and Trump shared many voters' darkest fears and prejudices. Cranmore is a genuinely decent and, as pols go, honest person. And I suspect that Jack Canterbury may actually believe his nostalgic rhetoric about a brave America of yester-year."

***

As I stared at the tangled web of pasta on my plate and reflected upon my own words, words from my past, I feigned lack of interest in the extraordinary politician sitting next to me. I had been studying propaganda for years. I had lectured and written many articles and books about it. I had taught thousands of students how to spot it. I thought I knew every trick in the book -- and yet Hernandez had completely fooled me.

I looked over at him as he gazed out the door at the people walking by on the sidewalk. I felt my hand make a fist. That bastard, lying politician had fooled me! I, of all people, had fallen for his regular, hard-working, straight-talking, neighbor-you-can-leave-the-keys-with, good-guy act. And I didn't like being fooled. Not one bit -- I hated it!

But I also couldn't help admiring him for his skill. I considered another line from Machiavelli:

"…our experience has been that those princes who have done great things have held good faith of little account, and have known how to circumvent the intellect of men by craft…"

Mr. Smith, my ass. This son-of-a-bitch sitting next me was a world-class bull-shit artist!

A man after my own heart.

Chapter Four

Hernandez' phone rang again. It was an aide, perhaps a speechwriter. They chatted and joked a bit, and then arranged to meet at the main entrance of the FAO, the Food and Agriculture Organization of the United Nations, which is headquartered in Rome. Hernandez, it seemed, was in town to give a speech there on sustainable agriculture. I wondered why. The usual reason pols speak at these international events is to polish their foreign policy credentials before an election. But he was fresh off a landslide win and had five years left in his Senate term.

"Right, Weeny-face," he said to his aide. "See you at the Director General's office at 11 AM. Unless you want to come over at 10:30 and blow me first. OK, 11 it is. Oh, and Douchebag? You're an idiot. You're fired. See you at 11."

He hung up, grinning at his own sophomoric humor. I had seen it before – immaturity, like mendacity, was something close to a job requirement for politicians.

I sipped my wine, observing him. I considered how a con-artist like him would hate getting exposed – almost as much as I hated the fact that he had conned me. The urge to wipe that stupid smirk off his face – and show him who was the boss – was irresistible.

"Excuse me, Senator Hernandez?" I leaned toward the flimflam man and smiled as innocently as I could. "Did I hear you're giving a speech at the FAO?"

I reached over his table and gave him my hand. He took it charily, no doubt wondering who I was and how much of his indecorous phone conversations I had heard. He stared at me expressionless as the waiter slipped a sliced melon with prosciutto under our outstretched arms, filled his glass, and wished him *"buon appetito."* I held onto his hand for several seconds, asserting my control.

"Marco Vannicelli," I beamed. "An honor to meet you, Senator. Are you in Rome just for the FAO, or will you have time for sightseeing?"

He forced a tepid smile in my direction but seemed at a loss for words. I loosened my grip, knowing he would pull his hand back as soon as I did. He immediately picked up his fork and knife, as if he might defend himself with them.

"How rude of me," I said. "I should let a gentleman enjoy his lunch in peace."

"Uh, no. That's …fine." He grinned meekly, reminding me of a puppy that had been caught peeing on the floor. He gazed down at his *prosciutto e melone.* Then he spun back toward me, and with a big, confident grin said: "A pleasure to meet you, Mr. Vannicelli. So, are you also in Rome for the FAO Summit?"

Of course: that's what a skillful politician would do. Caught with your pants down? Pull 'em up, pretend like nothing happened, and return to your script. Well-played, Hernandez, I thought. Too bad for you that you don't know whom you're playing with.

"I'm writing a policy paper," I lied, "on FAO's sustainable agriculture initiatives. What exactly will you be speaking about, Senator?"

His eyes lit up with what looked like fear, or at least discomfort. "Well, um, on sustainable…" he mumbled something incomprehensible as his voice trailed off. He stared at his plate and started pulling absently on the prosciutto with his fork and knife.

I looked up to the balcony behind him and I again imagined Mussolini strutting back and forth, spewing hateful lies about foreigners, as he flattered 20th century Italians with nostalgic nonsense about the glories of the Roman Empire. The dictator was no historian, but he knew that the masses were at least as ignorant as he was. He knew, as all demagogues throughout time have known, that the truth doesn't matter, so long as you state your lies confidently and repeatedly.

A master propagandist like Mussolini could get away with anything – and so could I. I leaned forward and showed Hernandez a toothy sneer: "So, Senator, have you read the studies projecting more climate-induced food shortages? And what about that FAO report concluding that global population has already outrun sustainable food production?" I had no idea what I was talking about, but I was sure he didn't either.

His phone rang, giving him the chance to escape. Hernandez asked the caller to meet him at his hotel, hung up, and politely told me that he had to go, extending his hand. His palm was sweaty, but as he rose, he managed another big, winning smile – he had terrific, straight white teeth. He left his lunch and wine on the table, hailed the waiter and pressed his thumb against the man's phone screen. As he moved toward the sidewalk, I asked if I could interview him for my paper. Instead of answering, he waved, saying that perhaps we might continue our conversation at the FAO reception.

Indeed, we might, I thought, as I watched him march away.

The waiter came over and cleared his table. I looked up and again beheld the balcony and visualized Mussolini. His hand rose in a Fascist salute. I heard the roar of cheering crowds.

Chapter Five

As fate would have it, the United Nations Food and Agricultural Organization building was commissioned by Mussolini in the 1930s to be the seat of Italy's Ministry for the Colonies. It consists of four massive white rectangles where several thousand people fight hunger mainly by going out for two-hour Roman lunches – presumably the fight against global malnutrition begins by setting a good example. No matter where it was, the FAO complex would be an eyesore. But the FAO is surrounded by so many of Rome's architectural wonders, right next to the Aventine and Palatine hills, the Circus Maximus and the glorious Baths of Caracalla – making Mussolini's aesthetic insult an offense not only to the eye, but also to the soul.

I arrived around 10:30 AM, as the Summit was opening, hoping to figure out how to get in. It was easier than I thought. The three guards at the entry were attending to a young American woman who had no press pass but claimed she was a journalist. As the Romans encircled her, a group of FAO employees walked by, flashing their credentials casually. One of the guards turned briefly and nodded to them. I slipped in with the group and lost myself among the people climbing the stairs to the main conference room, where the Director General had already begun his welcome speech.

I sat at the back of the room and looked around at the crowd of government ministers and their top aides. Well-dressed people of every size, shape and color sat politely, serious expressions on their faces as they pretended to listen to the Director General's solemn call for international action to prevent another global food crisis:

"We can accomplish what we came here to do," the DG said. "To ensure that every nation – every adult and every child – will be free of hunger. In this room, today my friends, history is to be made. It is ours to make. And our children and their children will thank us, as I thank you."

Polite applause followed this bullshit.

The next speaker was slow to arrive, so the clapping faded into the hum of whispered conversations. Then there was renewed polite applause as US Senator Dick Hernandez came to the podium. He had gotten a haircut since yesterday, and looked almost handsome, in a black designer suit skillfully altered to conceal his paunch. Hernandez looked out at the crowd as the invisible teleprompter brought up his speech. He smiled a warm, friendly smile, thanked the delegates for their welcome, and then loosened them up with a silly joke and the usual flattery before getting into the meat of his speech:

"Friends, I now need to say something important." He paused. His eyes pleaded. He took his time. The audience of dignitaries fell silent.

Nice touch, I thought. Good rhythm. This guy's got potential: great body language, understands how to use personal warmth, humor and praise to disarm skeptics. And he should patent that smile.

"I have such admiration," he continued, "for the Food and Agriculture Organization, and for your Director General, under whose able leadership we have seen impressive increases in global food production. FAO has helped diffuse new agricultural technologies, and those advances have enabled us to feed a hungry world. Billions of people are being fed today because of the great work of FAO and of the national leadership of people like you, present here today at this distinguished gathering."

His fawning was a bit obvious. I would have said it differently – but it did the trick.

"However, my friends, we need to step back and ask ourselves a troubling question."

He paused again for effect. His timing was excellent – the audience was all his. Not bad – with a little coaching this guy would be able to give a really great speech.

"And that question is whether, in the mid-21st century, with a global population of nine billion, we have run up against the limits of what technology can do for us."

Whispering punctured the silence. Some of the delegates seemed displeased by this reference to population. Hernandez continued:

"We must face reality. The human species is at grave risk of outrunning its food supply. If population continues to increase, we could face another global food shortage soon. Neo-Malthusians say food production actually drives population growth – that is a debatable matter. But what is no longer debatable is that we will lose the fight against hunger if we don't slow global population growth."

As soon as Hernandez spoke these words, the whispers grew louder, and two delegates got up and left the room.

"I realize that many of you do not agree with me, and you may feel it is patronizing for a Westerner to lecture you on this delicate topic. But we are running out of time. We need to take action now or we place the world in grave danger."

Whispers turned to grumbles, but Hernandez pressed on:

"Look at a few facts:

"First, food production has grown vastly, but there are as many hungry people today as there were in the 1950s.

"Second, to feed a population projected to rise to 9.6 billion by 2050, food production would have to increase at even a faster rate in the coming years.

"Third, a growing body of research suggests we may not be able to accomplish this. Cropland and pasture already well exceed half of the world's arable land, and food production is the most important source of ecosystem degradation and biodiversity loss. Agriculture accounts for over 15% of global greenhouse gas pollution, and at least 75% of the world's forests have been destroyed or damaged by humans.

"And finally – perhaps most alarmingly – most of the world's wild fisheries have collapsed because of over-fishing, pollution, and climate change…"

Oh Jesus, Hernandez! I thought, slumping in my chair. Know your audience! Agriculture ministers don't want to hear this environmentalist laundry list! What the hell was your speechwriter thinking?

Hernandez continued: "We need to look reality in the face, my distinguished friends, and see that increasing food production is only half of the challenge. Feeding the world sustainably – and avoiding another global food catastrophe…"

A hand came down on my shoulder. The middle-aged guard looked at me unkindly with dark brown Italian eyes, and gestured at my chest, where I should have had a guest pass. I rose apologetically, and tried to look as remorseful as I could as he accompanied me out the door and down the stairs to the street.

"Please don't come in without a pass again, sir. The summit is for invited guests only. It's not open to the public." He spoke American English well.

"I won't," I assured him in Italian, with a friendly smile. I complemented him on his excellent English, and he smiled back. In part to help save face, in part because I was getting hungry, I asked if there was a restaurant nearby that he would recommend.

"*Er Buco de' Mauro*. Fifteen minutes." He gestured toward the Roman Forum. "Turn right after the Coliseum. Tell them Antonio sent you. They'll treat you well." He smiled. "Remember the name – 'Antonio.'"

I wandered past the Circus Maximus and the Coliseum, thinking of the folly – or courage – that Hernandez had shown in bringing up population to that audience. His point about sustainable food production was accurate, but the way he did it was impolitic. He obviously had balls – and someone working for him who knew policy. But his speechwriter was tone deaf.

Chapter Six

The sun was high, and I was sweaty and hungry when I rounded the Coliseum and turned right toward the basilica of San Clemente, as the guard had advised me. There it was: *Er Buco de' Mauro* – a hole-in-the-wall restaurant on a tourist-free side street. It looked promising. Of course, finding a good restaurant in Rome is about as hard as finding a priest at the Vatican.

I walked down the steps to the small terrace and sat in the corner where the shadow of the building blocked the sun's rays. The sidewalk was just above my head, and I could hear the cars and smell the exhaust of the old petrol vehicles that, incredibly, were still legal in Italy. I changed tables to get some distance from the street, but I still could hear footsteps and conversations from the sidewalk above. A gray-haired older woman who had entered behind me smiled as she sat down at a table across the terrace, making a gesture indicating she understood why I had moved. I grinned back.

A tan, slender young waitress came over and sighed, lest I fail to appreciate how bored she was. She was trying to look sexy, I supposed, in her short black skirt, but her white blouse hung like a burlap sack around her neck and was moist around her armpits. She brought me a bottle of mineral water and a small carafe of house white wine without asking, and then started away without taking my order. I guessed that I had an hour before the sun cleared the rooftops and deprived me of my shade, so I called her back, asked what was good, and ordered right away. I tried, in vain, to cheer her up with a friendly comment about the heat. The smell of grilled calamari made me salivate, so I was happy when she brought me my appetizer of raw marinated anchovies sprinkled with red pepper and parsley. I thought of my mother and the marvels that came so effortlessly from her kitchen. The anchovies – even though they must have been farmed – were superb, and the bread was fresh. I was, for the moment, at peace with the world.

A woman and a man walked by on the sidewalk above, speaking loudly in English. I could see only their shoes and lower legs as they approached. They stopped just above my head, forcing me to listen as their conversation got angrier:

"What the bloody hell did you think you were doing, Randy? Why must you be such a slave to your stupid polling?" Her accent was English, and she enunciated like a BBC correspondent. I could see only her feet, but judging from her red Gucci shoes, I expected that the rest of her was as elegant as her voice.

"Look Kate. I don't make the polls up. The data say what they say. And, by the way, it's 'stupid,' not 'sty-oopid.'" He had an American accent, and he wore brown loafers that needed a shine. The bottoms of his jeans were worn and frayed at his heals.

"Well fuck you and your styooo-oo-pid data! I've been around this business long enough to know that polls don't tell you everything. Does it ever occur to any of you tossers that your 'data' just tell you what people think they might possibly think about things they've never thought much about, and about which they couldn't care less? It's bloody bollocks, Randy!"

She hesitated a moment before continuing.

"Look, just get out of here and leave me alone. I need to put on my happy face and calm him down. He's going to be really pissed off. One more screw-up like this…" she hesitated again. "Don't worry, I'll stand up for you. But get out of here before I change my mind!"

Mr. Scruffy Brown Loafers walked away silently, and "Kate" with the Guccis stayed where she was, while I returned to my anchovies. As I finished them, and my tonnarelli with tuna arrived, she started to shuffle and tap her feet impatiently. After a few minutes, she seemed to tire of the waiting and descended to the restaurant.

At the bottom of the stairs, as she reached the terrace and before I could see her face, she turned toward the pleasant older woman's table. Kate was tall and slender, with thick brown hair that fell lightly over her shoulders. Her movements were smooth and graceful, and her erect posture reminded me of Katherine Hepburn. The older woman's face lit up with pleasure and she smiled as Kate approached.

"Ciao Mamma, Sei già arrivata!"

Interesting, I thought as I dug into my pasta. Gucci Kate was Italian – although her English was so fluent and unaccented, she must have studied in England. The older woman was her mother. I thought of my chance meeting with Hernandez the day before, and his surprising Italian language skills.

I had not seen Kate's face yet, but I could tell from the graceful way she carried herself that she was confident and classy. She wore the same colors as the waitress, but there the resemblance ended: Kate's white skirt and black blouse fit her perfectly, and she seemed impossibly cool and comfortable for one who had been standing in the sun on a hot Roman afternoon.

Kate's mother rose slightly, and they kissed each other on both cheeks and began chatting in Italian, as the younger woman sat down. They gazed into each other's eyes and caressed one another's hair. Kate wore little makeup and no jewelry except for her wedding band, but she had bright green eyes and a smile that could raise the dead. I imagined she was in her mid-forties. Her mother called her "Caterina."

I returned to my tonnarelli. The tuna sauce was flavorful but subtle, with just a touch of capers. For a moment I forgot about the two women across the terrace as I savored my meal. The waitress, apparently concerned that I might enjoy my food in peace, turned on the Stream monitor on the wall directly opposite my table – thereby forcing me to watch two fools arguing about the safety of genetically modified food crops. A young man wearing a Greenpeace Italia t-shirt was saying that "Franken-foods" caused cancer, while another man wearing a suit claimed that there were no environmental risks from his company's new herbicide-resistant GMO crops. I couldn't decide which of them was the bigger idiot. I rose to shut the monitor off, but the waitress hissed at me. I smiled insincerely as I picked up the remote and turned down the volume before retreating to my table.

A taxi stopped above me, and I looked up. The windows opened, and the car specified the fare in multiple languages, before thanking its passengers in English. I saw the feet of two men getting out. One of them rushed toward the restaurant steps, while the other walked in the opposite direction to cross the street. The one who descended slowed as he reached the terrace, and he walked hesitantly over to Kate and her mother. He was young, short, fair-skinned and blond, and had an apologetic look on his homely face. Kate stared at him.

"Randy, what are you doing here? I told you to let me deal with it!"

"He saw me on the street and made me get in the cab. I'm sorry Kate, I…"

Randy looked over his shoulder up the stairs as Kate and her mother beamed at the large man in the black designer suit who was descending and placing a package of cigars into his pocket. The man walked past Randy without looking at him, straight over to the two ladies. He kissed each twice, gave a friendly wink to the older woman, and sat down. Randy was left standing awkwardly at the end of the table. No one invited him to sit. Dick Hernandez turned around, looking for the waitress.

Everything fell together in my mind. So, this BBC-English Kate person must be Catherine Richards Hernandez, the constitutional law professor at Georgetown. And – who knew? – she was also Italian. Randy, clearly, was Hernandez' pollster.

What a coincidence, I thought, that I should run into Hernandez again so soon.

Especially since I don't believe in coincidences.

Chapter Seven

"So, what the hell is a neo-Malpensian anyway? Those FAO-sters really busted my balls over that one!" Hernandez then paused and deadpanned: "Guess it was what the French might call a *'FAO pas.'*" He was relaxed and chuckling. Kate looked surprised at his good mood.

"It's not neo-Malpensian, dummy. Malpensa is an airport in Milan." She ran her finger over his forehead, as if to fix his hair, even though it already was in place. "You really aren't the sharpest knife in the drawer, now are you, Senator husband of mine?"

Randy, who was still standing awkwardly behind Hernandez explained, "It's neo-Malthusian, sir. Neo-Malthusians believe that population growth already has outrun sustainable global food produc…."

"Shut up, would you, Randy?" Hernandez didn't turn around – his eyes were fixed on Kate. "I don't care what it means. Just warn me next time if you are going to have me say shit that pisses everyone off, got it? Who gives a flying fuck what a neo-Malaysian is anyway?"

"Malthusian, sir. Malthus was an early 19th century econom…"

Hernandez spun around in his chair and glared at him.

"It won't happen again, sir."

"Sit the fuck down and shut the fuck up."

"Thank you, sir." Randy sat down quickly, behind Kate's mother, as if he might use her as a shield against further abuse. The older woman turned toward him and patted his hand kindly, as if to reassure him that everything would be OK. She introduced herself, in heavily accented English, as "Grazia." She then turned her back on him and asked Hernandez, in Italian, how his speech at FAO had gone. Before he could answer, Kate interjected that she thought it had gone well.

"Of course it didn't go well," Hernandez corrected her. Then he switched to English: "You know they hated it. But who the fuck cares? Asian agriculture ministers don't vote in American primary elections."

"Dammit Dick!" Kate placed her hands on her hips and leaned toward him. "I'm not going to ask you again – stop using the f-word in public!" She tried to take the edge off of the reprimand by wrinkling her nose, but then she let him have it: "I agreed to play the good political spouse. But you need to take this campaign seriously too! Otherwise, we're wasting everyone's time. Clean up that potty mouth of yours before someone records you, and all our efforts go down the drain!"

Hernandez said nothing. He turned to smile at Grazia, who nodded back. Randy looked nervously at the floor.

The waitress arrived, placed a liter of white wine and a bottle of sparkling mineral water on their table, and moved away. Hernandez watched her ass as she walked toward the kitchen – prompting Kate to take his head in her hands and forcibly turn his face toward her.

"She seems nice," Hernandez grinned stupidly.

Kate chuckled and shook his face affectionately: "So naturally you thought it appropriate to stare at her bum?"

"Poor girl, working her ass off in this heat!" he laughed, before calling the woman over. She scowled from across the room, but grabbed a menu and brought it to him. He observed it thoughtfully for at least a minute, humming, while she tapped her feet impatiently. Kate snatched the menu from him and ordered farfalle with salmon for everyone, without asking their preferences. She handed the menu back to the waitress and asked her to bring a second liter of sparkling water.

Family chatter in Italian followed, leaving Randy alone with his phone at the end of the table. I understood from the conversation that Grazia had not seen them for some months. When Kate announced that Dick was going to run for President, Grazia smiled and said she was pleased to hear it.

"You will be a great President, Riccardino," she said, with what sounded like genuine affection. "When Caterina first brought you home, I knew you were special. So smart and polite – and I was impressed how you made an effort to speak Italian. Not like most American students in Italy."

So, Hernandez had been an exchange student in college. Not exactly the up-from-poverty story I had heard, but it explained his Italian.

Hernandez turned toward Randy and barked something at him, but I couldn't make out what he said, because a truck drove by on the cobblestones above my head just at that moment.

Randy sat up straight: "Senator Hernandez, you pay me for my best political advice. I intend to give it to you, even if it hurts." He sat even straighter, as if impressed by his own effort at assertiveness. Hernandez said nothing, but Kate gave Randy a look suggesting that his head was in imminent danger of getting bitten off. He persisted:

"Look, I know you want to run as 'The Environmentalist Candidate.' But my polls and focus groups say it won't work. Even with the climate and food crises, the floods and wildfires, despite the dead fish and dead lakes and green flies, American voters consistently rank the environment somewhere behind bedbugs and hemorrhoids in terms of their main areas of concern." He smiled at his own attempted joke. Hernandez did not. "The environment alone won't get you to the White House, sir. We need to link it to issues voters care more about, like jobs and immigration. That's why we did the FAO speech. My data show that low-information voters for some reason think population growth drives illegal immigration. We'll show a clip to our focus groups and see if it moves anything."

Hernandez turned his back on Randy without saying a word. The pollster tried not to look deflated by this snub, but when Hernandez asked Kate, in Italian, what she thought, Randy slouched into his seat. Kate hesitated, before saying, in English, that she thought Randy might be right. I had the impression that she was motivated more out of pity than conviction.

As she struggled for words, I saw my opening. My dessert had just arrived, but I put down my fork and walked across the terrace toward their table. The waitress seemed concerned that I was neglecting my tiramisù, but I had something important to do. I shut off the annoying monitor as I passed it. By the time I got to the Hernandez table, all four of them were looking at me. Grazia and Randy looked confused, but Dick and Kate were smiling. I greeted them and asked if I could join. Hernandez did not hesitate:

"Mr. Vannicelli! How nice to see you again. Have a seat! Really, what a pleasure this is!"

"The pleasure, Senator, is all mine. I have some thoughts on political messaging that I would like to share with you."

Chapter Eight

"Please sit down, Mr. Vannicelli. I've been looking forward to this moment," Hernandez gestured toward the seat across from him and Kate. Grazia and Randy regarded me with curiosity. Kate's look was something between friendly and triumphant.

"You had me followed, Senator," I stated matter-of-factly as I sat.

Hernandez pointed at his chest with both hands, feigning surprise. "You're a smart guy, aren't you, Mr. Vannicelli? You may not know shit about sustainable agriculture, or those neo-Marsupials or whatever they are, but I know talent when I see it. That's why I keep this douchebag Randy around."

Hernandez nodded in Randy's direction, but kept his gaze fixed on me. Randy smiled.

"He only looks and acts like a moron. In reality, he's the best pollster in the business."

Randy seemed genuinely pleased at this comment, but when I grinned at him, the corners of his mouth descended to a neutral position.

"After our chance meeting yesterday, we did some research on you, Mr. Vannicelli." Hernandez said.

"Call me Marco."

Hernandez obviously thought very highly of himself – I hoped inviting him to a first-name basis might take him down a notch, but he didn't miss a beat: "At first, Marco, I thought you might have been working for Cranmore, but we found out you are just one very smart, and very unemployed, expert on propaganda."

"We even read a bit of your work," Kate smiled. "Your article on how propaganda uses archetypal myths was intriguing. Really quite interesting."

Hernandez paused for my reaction, but I gave him only a Mona Lisa smile. He continued: "I trust you won't tell anyone that my man Antonio impersonated an FAO guard, will you? That could be embarrassing."

I recalled the face of the Italian guard who had escorted me out the door, and, looking up, I saw the same man descending the stairs. He nodded in my direction as he moved toward Hernandez. The man spoke Italian, but with an American accent. Standing at the end of the table, he faced his boss, but his words were meant for me:

"I imagine the Senator has explained why we're all here, Mr... or should I say 'Professor' Vannicelli?"

"Not yet, but I think I have an idea." I smiled before adding, "And 'Professor' will do just fine."

"We thought it might be nice to have lunch together. To get to know one another. That's why I sent you here. Professor."

"Lunch?" I asked. "To get to know one another? You sent me here?" I noticed his use of the word "we," as if he were more important that he probably was. Antonio struck me as one of those hacks that politicians bring along with them to perform tasks that don't require an excess of any particular talent.

Still facing Hernandez, he continued his recount of what he imagined to be an act of genius: "You asked if I knew of a good restaurant, so I sent you here." He turned toward me. "I passed it on the way this morning. Never been. How's the food?" he asked, perhaps expecting to see admiration on my face. I offered a faint smile and my hand, which he took briefly before sitting. Randy hesitated before making room for him.

Kate whispered something in Dick's ear, observing me with intelligent eyes. Remembering who she was – a constitutional law professor – I wondered if she, not her wise-ass, arrogant husband, might be the smartest one in the room.

I turned toward them and got right to the point: "So Senator, I listened to your speech."

"How was it? Oh, and call me Dick."

"It sucked, Dick. It was a pathetic failure." He stared at me, but then cracked a smile. Everyone else looked at me like I was insane.

"Truly a pathetic failure," I continued. "It lacked pathos. There was no emotive narrative, no appeal to the audience's feelings. It was a litany of facts and data, with no heart. No offense, Senator, but as a speech it was dead-on-arrival."

I noticed Randy shaking his head, but Hernandez looked unperturbed. "I never expected them to *like* the speech. That isn't why I gave it." Randy and Kate exchanged glances. "What do I care what a bunch of foreign bureaucrats and politicians think? Pissing off faceless UN types is good politics in middle America. Isn't that right, Randy?" Hernandez looked to his pollster.

Randy sat up. "Well actually, I wouldn't say that. Over 90% of likely Democratic primary voters support the United Nations. So, I don't see…"

"Of course, you don't see." Hernandez interrupted. "Because you're a moron. Most voters know nothing about the UN, and they couldn't care less about it. But 10% heard on Fox News that the UN is an international conspiracy to make us all gay-marry and speak Esperanto. Or some such shit. Those are the only voters who care about the UN. And they're a bunch of ignorant rednecks that don't like anyone who isn't an ignorant redneck fuck-head just like them. Pissing off a UN crowd of douchebag fuckface quiche-eating foreigners…"

Kate cleared her throat. Dick turned toward her and smiled. She managed a look that simultaneously validated her husband's argument while admonishing him for his profanity.

"So," I asked, "you were deliberately annoying a UN audience, so that you could move to the environmentalist left later without being accused of being an un-American internationalist?"

Randy interjected before Hernandez could answer my question: "We were trying, Mr. Vannicelli" – he spoke my name slowly and shook his head to highlight how stupid he considered my question – "to see if we could move the needle by linking Dick's environmentalism to anti-immigrant fears. Our polling…."

"Please excuse me – Randy, is it? But I don't care what your polling says. What is your narrative?" He shrank back.

"What is your narrative?" I asked again.

Randy looked confused, but Dick and Kate were staring at me attentively.

"What is your narrative, Randy? What's the *story* you're telling? Who do your voters think they are in that story? Who is your candidate in that story, other than some guy pissing off some UN bureaucrats?"

"Not to mention the neo-Mamma's Boys," Hernandez chuckled. "Look, I get what you are saying. You're saying I need to establish my image before I start talking about policies. Do you get that, Randy?" The pollster glowered back.

"Repeat after me, Randy: 'I don't understand a fucking thing. Because I'm a dumb shithead.'"

"I'm a dumb shithead, sir."

Hernandez continued: "So you want me to start with my image and..."

I interrupted him: "No Senator, your image is Step Three. Your image is the guy the voter identifies with and can trust to solve the voter's problem. But that comes only after Step Two, which is establishing what the problem is, and making sure the voter sees it as their own personal problem, as something they care about. And before you can do that, you need to take Step One, which is to tap into a narrative that makes sense to the voter: What is this all about? What myths and legends are you addressing? Voters have stories in their minds, from Goldilocks, to Baby Jesus, to Honest Abe, to the Little-Engine-That-Could. They have hopes and dreams. Archetypal heroes and villains. Most voters don't understand or care about policy. They want bedtime stories. Things make sense to them only if they fit into some compelling, familiar narrative. What is the story in their minds that you are speaking to?"

Their faces were expressionless. I thought I had lost them, but then Hernandez spoke:

"America the beautiful." He turned toward Kate and smiled as he spoke. "From sea to shining sea. Purple mountains majesty. The towering Rockies, rivers filled with salmon, fields of golden grain. A pristine gift of the Almighty that provides sustenance to the nation and makes America the breadbasket of the world – all of it at risk because of greed. Because some people don't care about God's gift. They want to allow mining companies to destroy this gift to all of us, to benefit the few. Greedy corporations that don't care if we leave our children a ruined, unlivable planet. They think the people are too stupid to see what they are doing."

Hernandez got it. Totally. And the look on Kate's face told me that she was right there with him. She threw her arms around her husband and beamed at me: "I told you we should meet him!"

I nodded.

Dick laughed as he sat back and put his arms behind his head and his feet on the table. He began singing: "Oh give me a home, where the buffalo roam, where the deer and the antelope hump each other…"

Grazia tried not to look appalled at this display of bad American manners. The waitress came over and began serving them as she winced with disgust. Randy and Antonio looked blankly at each other.

Kate swept Dick's feet off the table, with a smile on her face, and leaned forward toward me.

"I like this guy!" she said, smiling at me while hugging Dick. "I really like this guy!"

PART TWO

*The prince who would accomplish great things
must know how to deceive.*

— Machiavelli

*He looked out the window as twilight descended on the Rose Garden. His eyes followed
a shadow creeping toward him.*

"Do me a favor, Marco?"

"A favor, Mr. President?"

*"I know you need to leave. But..." Hernandez stopped for a moment; his voice was
cracking... "I want you to write one more speech before you go."*

"Sir?"

*"The speech where I reluctantly accept your resignation, and I lay the praise on
embarrassingly thick? The speech where I explain how much I have learned from you,
how much you have contributed to the administration. And how much you will be
missed."*

He paused.

*"Because I wouldn't be here if it were not for you, my friend." His eyes were moist,
but he was smiling.*

*"Yes, Mr. President." I nodded. "Of course, and..." I had to stop for a moment to
compose myself, "And I'm sorry I told you to go to hell. That was uncalled for. I could
have said it better..."*

*"No problem. I knew this was coming, and I understand you need to move on.
We're going to miss you a lot around here, but Kate and I respect your decision."*

There was a kind look in his eyes. Kate, standing by the window, nodded. She had seen it too.

"It's been an honor to serve you. But yes, I do need to go. I'll send you the speech tonight." I started toward the door.

"The honor has been mine. Marco. You're…"

I turned back toward him, and we looked into each other's eyes.

"What I'm trying to say is…"

"Sir?"

"You're more than just a trusted and talented aide. You're also my friend – and I'm really, really going to miss you."

"Thank you, Dick. I'll miss you too. And if there ever is an emergency and you…"

"And you have been my teacher."

"It won't be the same without you…" Kate said.

Hernandez rose from the behind the Resolute Desk, walked to me, and gave me a hug. Kate put her hand on my shoulder. The three of us turned toward the Rose Garden and watched the last green flies of the day tapping on the window. They would be gone for the night soon, but back in the morning. I would not be.

I shook the President's hand and gave the First Lady one last hug before turning and walking out the door of the Oval Office. My back felt better.

Chapter Nine

He strode confidently to the podium. The sun was shining, and the wind gently fluffed his black hair. The Grand Canyon behind him was the perfect visual. We had decided on jeans, cowboy boots and an open collar, but no hat or bolo tie. Kate and Alexandra stood behind him, holding hands, and wearing the same white cowboy boots, long country skirts and sleeveless white blouses, except that Kate's skirt was blue and Alexandra's was red. Periodically they turned and faced each other and smiled, as we had rehearsed. The band played a soft, jazzy "America the Beautiful," that disappeared into the vastness of the Canyon behind the stage. The perfect First Family swayed to the music.

He knew what he had to do. I had written one hell of a speech – if I don't mind saying so myself – and we had practiced it until he had it perfect. Randy was in the limo, crunching numbers on his computer. I stood just offstage. Kate winked at me. She looked incredibly fresh for someone who had just gotten off a plane from London.

Nobody thought we had a chance of catching Cranmore, but the media were all there. Even Fox News. They had been ridiculing Hernandez for years – alternatively calling him "Mr. Clean" and "Senator Tree-hugger," while chuckling derisively at whatever he said. As in "So Senator Tree-hugger thinks Americans are wasteful gluttons. Hey, Mr. Clean! Some of us have to drive to work! Does that make us bad people? Or is it because of your so-called (snicker, snicker) '*anthropogenic* – ooh what a big word! – global warming?' Some people think it's because Senator Tree-Hugger hates America. What do you think?"

You had to admit their logic was unassailable.

But the talking heads, even at Fox, were desperate for a good race. On the Republican side they had nothing – the only person running against Jack Canterbury was that lunatic Zaricki, a former Klansman who said Moses had come to him in a dream and asked him to run to protect the Second Amendment which, it would seem, was somehow also one of the Ten Commandments.

So, the cameras were there to take our message to the country. The crowd of environmental activists applauded enthusiastically, practically jumping out of their Birkenstocks. Hernandez waited, smiling his famous friendly smile. The music softened, allowing him to stand briefly before the crowd in near silence, the wind blowing through the canyon. Then he began, with that pensive tone we had practiced – his voice cracking so very subtly with wonder and awe as he began:

"My Friends! Look – just look! – at this magnificent canyon behind me!"

He lifted both his arms high, like a preacher – make that like Jesus on the Mount – and said nothing more. He smiled the magic smile again, and then he waited for the applause to begin and reach its crescendo. Once it did, he broke into it like a surfer breaking into a wave:

"America is blessed with so many natural wonders. This Grand Canyon. Yosemite, Yellowstone, the Great Smokey Mountains, the Presidential Range in New Hampshire, and so many more. These wonders are our cathedrals, my fellow Americans. They are our pride and our heritage."

He paused again, smiled again, waited again. And then an almost imperceptible look of worry came across his face. We had practiced it. Perfect!

"These gifts are ours to enjoy..." He lowered his voice slightly, nodding knowingly: *"...but also to protect. To RESPECT. To preserve for our children and their children. These gifts are unique, irreplaceable. And because of the wisdom of national leaders who came before us, like Teddy Roosevelt and FDR and JFK..."*

We needed a majority of Democrats, of course – and who cared if Carter had done more for the environment than FDR and JFK put together? An icon is an icon.

"...they remain pristine, preserved for our children and their children. The wonders of this country enrich our lives. They fill our souls. They make us who we are."

He paused again, before saying clearly and softly and slowly: *"A-mer-icans!"*

The crowd applauded enthusiastically, but solemnly. He played them like a maestro.

"When I look out on this Canyon, I am reminded of the sad but beautiful words of Chief Seattle, responding to the US government's proposal to purchase Native American land in the 1840s."

He waited again, looked serenely out at the crowd, and continued:

"'How can you buy or sell the sky, the warmth of the land?' Chief Seattle asked. 'The idea is strange to us. If we do not own the freshness of the air and sparkle of the water, how can you buy them?

"'Every part of this earth is sacred to my people. Every shining pine needle, every sandy shore, every mist in the dark woods, every clearing, and every humming insect is holy in the memory and experience of my people. The sap which courses through the trees carries the memories....'"

I looked over the crowd and smiled. They seemed hypnotized. I knew the Native American trick would push their buttons.

"'So, when the Great Chief in Washington sends word that he wishes to buy our land, he asks much of us.

"'This we know: All things are connected. Whatever befalls the earth befalls the sons of the earth. Man did not weave the web of life; he is merely a strand in it. Whatever he does to the web, he does to himself....

"'When the last Indian has vanished from the earth, and his memory is only the shadow of a cloud moving across the prairie, these shores and forests will still hold the spirits of my people. For they love this earth as the newborn loves its mother's heartbeat.

"'So, if we sell our land, love it as we have loved it. Care for it as we have cared for it. Hold in your mind the memory of the land as it is when you take it. And preserve it for your children...'"

Hernandez then stood silent in reverence for a full 20 seconds, his palm against his chest, as we had rehearsed. The Grand Canyon behind him became one with the silence – I had bet Kate $10 that this image would be the one the networks used. Then he continued:

"My fellow Americans, let us always remember Chief Seattle's words. Let us swear to defend this land from those who do not understand its sacred value. Let us never soften in our resolve to protect America from shortsighted people who would violate her, who would scar her face, pollute her waters, poison her air for short-term gains.

"And let us never be fooled by those who claim, falsely, that our environment must be sacrificed for our prosperity. For we know that this is not true."

Dick paused again, before connecting the Indian Myth to his own Horatio Alger Story:

"Let me tell you a story. It is the story of a boy and his grandfather. The old man had come to this country when he was young, poor and afraid, speaking little English and having left everyone he knew. He wound up in a small town where he heard the rents were low and there were jobs for immigrants. After a few years of backbreaking work in the fields, he married and had a family. He and his wife worked hard for many more years. The family stuck together, had a few lucky breaks, and eventually they were able to buy a small store on the edge of a national park.

"Every morning early, before opening the store and sending his grandson off to school, the grandfather took the little boy's hand and they walked together along the rushing river behind their house, where it ran along the edge of the park. The river was beautiful in a different way every day. In the Spring, the rapids were high, and the current was powerful. In the Fall, the stream meandered calmly. In the winter, it froze over, but you could still hear the water beneath the ice. Above, in the national park, were towering, snow-capped peaks. Each day, the boy and his grandfather walked along the river's bank in silence. They said little, because there was little that needed to be said. They loved the river, and the mountains, the trees blowing in the wind, the meadows filled with elk. And they understood the importance of caring for what you love.

"Tourists came by the store asking if they could rent a canoe to shoot the rapids. So, the family borrowed some money to buy first one canoe, then two more. As a teenager, the boy took tourists on fly fishing tours on the river inside the park. He couldn't believe he could make a living doing something so enjoyable!

"When he was a bit older, he enrolled in the local community college, and then he went on to UCLA, where he majored in environmental studies. For him, making a

living and caring for nature went together. He knew that this beautiful, bountiful land would always take care of us, if we took care of it.

"The grandfather looked after the boy until their roles gradually reversed and the boy began looking after his aging grandfather. Toward the end, the boy – now a man – held his grandfather's hand gently at his bedside, sad that he was leaving, but full of gratitude for having known him. For having walked the river's bank with him all those years. When the old man passed, the young man cried. Of loss, but not of despair. His grandfather had given him such love and such strength that his passing was hard, but not unbearable. The young man knew that his grandfather would always walk alongside him. What he had given him could never be taken away. That young man continued to take long walks along the river and into the park. He never forgot the power of love, and he never forgot the restorative strength of the river, the mountains, the forests, the meadows. He walked by himself now, but never was he alone."

Hernandez halted briefly, with a soft, far-away look in his eyes. As he let his words settle, I noticed that Kate seemed on the verge of tears. I wiped a tear from my own cheek as Dick began again:

"That young man became an environmental activist, my friends. He fought many a good fight against the polluters and the despoilers. He fought those who wanted to drill and mine in our national forests, those who sought to run oil pipelines through sensitive wilderness areas, those who would put housing developments inside our national parks. He married, moved to the city, had a family of his own…."

On cue, Kate and Alexandra, both gorgeous and beaming, stepped forward, Kate on his right, Alexandra on his left, as he put his arms around them. The perfect, loving, all-American family.

Smiling ear to ear he continued: *"Friends, that guy somehow managed to marry the smartest, most beautiful woman he had ever met!"* The crowd started to cheer and clap knowingly. Kate, on cue, acted surprised and embarrassed *"…and they were blessed with a wonderful, talented, awesome daughter!"*

The applause intensified. Kate and Alexandra gazed with motherly-daughterly love, first at Hernandez, and then at each other, then back to him. Nice!

"He never forgot the lessons he had learned as a child. He ran for public office. He became a US Congressman and later head of the Environmental Protection Agency. And today, my friends, that man is a US Senator. Like you, he loves this country, and like you, he is committed to protecting this land and these skies from those who see America as a resource to exploit, rather than as a gift to cherish and protect. Like you, he believes that 'Real Americans' don't bow to the whims of corporate polluters with big checkbooks, small hearts, and short sight. 'Real Americans' don't crouch in fear. They don't run away from battles that need to be fought. 'Real Americans' defend their country from the polluters and the despoilers – including those who bankroll politicians!"

This jab at Jack Canterbury and his "Real Americans" crap had been Kate's idea. It worked – the crowd chuckled and clapped.

"My friends, I promise you that I will stand with you until my last day as we defend America together. I will remain true to the memory of my papito *and to the lessons of my youth!"*

By now the applause was constant, as we had intended.

"Today, my friends," he paused and smiled, *"I am here to announce that I am running to be your next President!"*

An explosion of applause almost drowned him out. He raised his voice and shouted above the cheers, catching the crowd's energy like a sail catching the wind:

"Do you stand with me, my friends, to defend this great country of ours?

Will you join me? We have a nation to protect. Will you join me?"

The crowd applauded and roared with cries of "Yes! Yes!"

"Do you say 'NO!' to those who would build roads and pipelines inside this great national park?"

Some people were shouting "NO!" while others were still shouting "Yes!"

Shit! My bad – I should have foreseen that! I made a mental note of it. But it didn't matter. Hernandez got it immediately and modified the remaining applause lines to whip them up into a frenzy of "YES!"

"Do you say 'Yes!' to sustainable tourism?"

"YES!"

"Do you say 'No!' to global warming and 'Yes!' to renewable energy?"

"YES!"

"Do you say 'No!' to drilling and 'YES!' to solar?"

"YES!"

And then finally, of course, the complete list of eco-buzzwords, in no particular order:

"Wind Power! Distributed generation! Biofuels! Sustainable Green jobs! Organic farming! Electric cars! Tidal Power!" The crowd was clapping and shouting 'YES!' madly.

"THIS is America's Prosperous Green Future! Walk with me, my friends. Walk with me, walk with my grandfather, along the mighty river that is America. Walk with me through great canyons and over majestic mountains! Walk with me as we honor and protect this blessed land!"

He paused and waited for the roar of the crowd to subside. When it did, he continued, in that somber tone we had decided on:

"My fellow Americans, let us walk with Chief Seattle. Let us walk with Teddy Roosevelt and FDR and Jack Kennedy. Let all of us who love America walk together. Arm in arm. Shoulder to shoulder. Together, my friends, we will stop the despoilers and the polluters. Together we will build a strong, prosperous and green future. We will protect and preserve our natural heritage, we will stop the climate crisis, and we will create millions of good, sustainable jobs for our people."

He paused briefly, and then continued, his voice slightly softer:

"Because we know that Chief Seattle was right: 'All things are connected. Whatever befalls the earth befalls the sons of the earth. Man did not weave the web of life; he is merely a strand in it. Whatever he does to the web, he does to himself.'

"Protecting America is our sacred obligation, my fellow citizens. Walk with me! Walk with me!"

The clapping began again. He hugged Kate and Alexandra and waited for the applause to reach its crescendo.

"Let us all walk together, my fellow Americans, toward a green and prosperous future. God bless you. God bless you all. And God bless the United States of America!"

The applause rose like Old Faithful as Hernandez, Kate and Alexandra beamed and waved.

Holy shit! That was good. We had nailed our environmentalist base to the floor. I needed a drink. I walked to the van, opened the cooler, grabbed a beer, and sat down on a bench facing the canyon. It was, indeed, a cathedral. A magnificent cathedral. I popped the beer bottle and admired the colors of the Grand Canyon.

"One for me too?" It was Alexandra. I handed the open beer to her, stepped back to the cooler, grabbed another for myself, and rejoined her on the bench.

"Good show, I guess," she said, gazing at the red, yellow, orange and purple tones of the canyon. "Too bad that's all it was. A show. And a fucking waste of everyone's time!" She rose and walked away.

Ah, to be young again, I thought. Before you figure out that it's all just a show.

Next stop Hollywood for some big liberal money.

Chapter Ten

The private jet to LA had been provided by Betty Rossi, who fancied herself not only a great actor (which, arguably, she was), but also an Italian-American in touch with her roots. Whenever I saw her, she would embrace me with what she thought was a typical effusive Italian greeting. You know, kisses on each cheek followed by some Neapolitan gibberish that only those who had come over on the same boat as her great-grandparents would understand? But, of course, I needed to play along, because after the kissing and the gibberish and some schmoozing with the Senator (who would pretend like he gave a mouse turd about her policy ideas) we expected a check and some lucrative introductions. I counted my blessings – Betty seemed to have a soft spot for Antonio, and no matter how he tried to avoid her, she always managed to corner him. He had told her repeatedly that he was from Brooklyn, not Naples, but she insisted on hugging him and calling him her "*cumpagno*," as he sneered politely.

Hernandez was slouching in the plane's first row, his feet against the bulkhead, page-winking through his Reader, and chuckling. We ignored the smell of marijuana coming from the loo – Kate had persuaded Alexandra to play the good daughter for the campaign, but in return, no one was to give her any crap about her pot smoking. She apparently also got to call Hernandez "Senator Douchebag Fucking Loser" all she wanted.

"What's so funny, Senator?" I asked. "What're you reading?"

"*Science Today*," he said absently, still snickering softly. I noticed his page-winks were left-eyed – typical, say the psychologists, of clairvoyants, empaths, mathematicians, philosophers, classical musicians, and psychopaths.

I gave up trying to talk to him, and walked toward Kate and Randy, who were watching CNN on the wall monitor. The blue line at the bottom of the screen indicated that real-time fact-checking found no falsehoods in what was being said.

Nian Zhen Cooper was interviewing a British scientist – a young, brown-haired woman talking about biotechnology. Kate and Randy turned briefly to look at each other, as if they knew the woman, before returning their gazes to the screen. The scientist was warning that international genetic engineering research protocols were so lax that it was only a question of "when, not if, we experience a major GMO invasive species incident."

Cooper ran tiny fingers through her short black hair as she tried to summarize the scientist's warning. "So, what you are saying is that recent advances in gene manipulation…"

"Yes…" the scientist interrupted Cooper "we need to get our act together – fast – and impose stronger – and global – controls on genetic manipulation. A really nasty bug or invasive plant could show up any day – and when it does, it'll be too late. Once an organism is in the wild, it's there forever. And a herbicide-resistant weed, for example, could wreak havoc on agriculture worldwide."

Cooper nodded. "Thank you for your time, Dr. Richards. In other news to-day…"

"Really, Nian Zhen." The scientist wasn't finished. "Please hear me out. Remember the antibiotic-resistant bacteria crisis? And before that, the Covid-19 coronavirus? Well, this could be even worse! Did you know…" The scientist's microphone suddenly went silent, and Cooper's image filled the screen.

"Thank you once again, Dr. Rachel Richards of London University. We hope to have you on our show again soon." Cooper turned toward the side-camera. "In other news today, two gentlemen who would be President, a Democrat and a Republican, threw their hats in the ring."

Hernandez looked up from his paper and turned toward the monitor just as footage of him at the Grand Canyon came up. He had his arms in the air – I pulled $10 out of my wallet and handed it to Kate. I expected some sort of victor's smile, but she looked past me, lost in thought, and absently dropped the bill into her purse.

The TV visual wasn't half bad – it was perfect in fact for "the Environmental Candidate." But Cooper damned us with faint praise, dismissing Hernandez as the "quixotic challenger on the Democratic side" – before turning to "the big news today that Jack Canterbury made it official. He's running for the Republican nomination."

Canterbury had the Republican race won before it began. All the Republican mega-donors had made an early deal to support him, and he seemed to have something for everyone: the religious right would get a constitutional amendment banning "Islamic law, secularist immorality, and mandatory transgenderism" (sin and temptation, it seems, were to remain legal at the federal level); the small government buffs would obtain privatization of Social Security; the war hawks would get withdrawal from the hypersonic missile treaty, the gun nuts would be allowed their 3D printers, and the cranky old xenophobes would get their silly border wall, which miraculously had risen like a vote-snatching phoenix from Trump's ashes. Most importantly, the GOP big boys had agreed to crush anyone who dared to challenge the Anointed One. So, the only Republican challenging Canterbury was that batshit crazy Zaricki, who was running because Moses, and now apparently also Jesus, had come to him in a dream.

CNN aired a full five minutes of Canterbury's speech. As there was little factual content to his rhetorical dribble, both the CNN's Truth-Gauge and the monitor's internal fact-checker held steady at "Zero," occasionally flashing "Opinion presented as Fact," but without any "Falsehood" alerts.

The speech was classic Jack Canterbury – sound and fury, signifying nothing. It was so dumb, I didn't know whether to laugh or cry. I also was confused: he had no serious opposition for the Republican nomination, so why wasn't he attacking President Cranmore? He never even mentioned her name. Instead, all he had was a string of insipid, patriotic slogans:

"...Let me tell you my friends, Real Americans aren't afraid. They believe in hard work and personal responsibility..."

Really? His focus groups said this twaddle still got the old geezers going?

"...Real Americans know that this is the most powerful, most respected country in the history of the world..."

Or at least it was before you-know-who Made It Great Again.

"...Real Americans don't appease. They stand their ground. They don't back down. They bow to no one..."

Because of arthritis?

"...A shining city on a hill. A guiding light for those who know that freedom isn't free..."

Why was he was pulling this old crap out of the rhetorical hopper, instead of attacking his opponent? Sally Cranmore had little to show for her years in the White House, but she was honest (her Crypto-rating was 98%, even higher than Dick's) and voters found her decency and common sense reassuring after the madness of the pre-Crisis and Crisis years. Jack Canterbury's only chance was to attack the President's lack of accomplishments. Why was he being such a poodle when the situation called for a mean, snarling Doberman?

I turned to Hernandez: "He's either an idiot, or he knows something we don't know."

The Senator ignored me and kept reading. The guy was incredible – he had just given the best speech of his life, the media was utterly dismissing him, and he was perusing a damn science journal!

A panel of talking heads came on. Hernandez continued reading while they analyzed the Canterbury candidacy:

"I just don't understand, Hien Zhen," one of them said, as if reading my mind. "Canterbury has no real opposition for the Republican nomination. There will be a Cranmore-Canterbury contest in the Fall, and she's far ahead in every poll. That won't change until he goes after her. He should be hitting her hard, taking her down a notch. But instead, all we hear is this 'Real Americans' rhetoric. And he certainly shouldn't expect much help from Senator Hernandez' quixotic effort."

"They call me 'quixotic' one more time and I'm going have to buy you a donkey, Vannicelli." Dick smiled, without looking up from his Reader. "What do you think, 'Sancho?'"

Randy snickered from behind his laptop. Kate smiled at me mercifully, but then turned and looked out the window at the clouds beneath us.

The talking head continued: "A boutique candidate like Senator Hernandez is no threat to a popular, incumbent President of his own party. He will make his point about the environment, and then he'll be gone by March, after Cranmore trounces him in the early primaries."

Hernandez kept reading. Kate turned back to the monitor, but she had a far-away look in her eyes as she told it to switch to Fox. The same footage of him at the Grand Canyon was looping behind that lying sleaze-bag Lester Downs, smiling at the camera like Wiley Coyote about to light a fuse labeled "Acme TNT." The monitor flashed "Low-Veri-rated Programming – Real-time Fact-check Auto-active" across the bottom of the screen. Downs was doing his usual Fox Full Monty: "So we can see here what he's up to, right? Senator Tree-Hugger Hernandez thinks Americans are so stupid that they can't see that the environmentalists are ruining our economy. It seems Mr. Clean wants us all to make our living as (snicker) fly-fishing guides..."

The monitor flashed "False!" across the screen as I got up to go to the bathroom, where Alexandra was emerging, followed by a cloud of pot smoke. The marijuana had reddened her eyes, but it had not relaxed her. She looked as annoyed and hostile as she had before going in fifteen minutes earlier. She smiled at me the way a store clerk smiles at you when you want to return something without a receipt. Running her fingers through her brown hair as she walked past me, she muttered something under her breath about her father being a "douchebag loser."

I looked back at Hernandez and saw that he was grinning like someone who had just found the keys to the kingdom. He reached out to his left and grabbed Kate, pulling her toward his Reader.

"You too! Come over here, Sancho!" he ordered, without looking up. I ignored him and continued toward the loo.

"Vannicelli! Marco! Come here! This is big. Huge!"

Chapter Eleven

Hernandez jumped up and down in his seat like a schoolboy who had just hacked the teacher's grading program. "Don't you see?!" he said, pointing at his Reader and shifting his gaze from it to Kate and back again. "This is it!"

He turned toward me, as I was about to enter the tiny bathroom at the back of the jet. "Marco! Get your ass over here!"

I needed to pee, but I turned around and started toward the front of the plane.

"Loser," Alexandra mumbled under her breath to no one in particular, as she stepped to where Antonio was napping and Randy was staring at his computer.

Hernandez shoved the tablet at me and Kate, who nodded tentatively with a wrinkled brow.

"See?" he said, pointing at the screen. "Genetically modified switchgrass. In Iowa and Missouri! GMO switchgrass, Marco! Damaging crops, Kate! When it spreads, farmers will lose money!"

"Who would have thought a rogue invasive species ruining people's livelihoods could produce such joy?" I thought as I read.

"OK," Kate said. "So, there's some nasty GMO switchgrass out there in..." Her eyes lit up. "... 'Iowa and Missouri?'" She smiled. "As in the first-round primary elections Iowa and Missouri?"

Hernandez beamed as they hugged each other. He kissed her cheek.

I finished scanning the article and looked up. They were staring at me, like puppies hoping for a treat. I looked at my watch.

"Give me a minute," I said as I grabbed my Reader.

***

"OK, Dick. Here's what you're going to say at Rossi's fundraiser." I tilted my Reader toward his. As he reached out, I snatched it back.

"We'll also do a press release, but you need to listen carefully…"

"So, let me see it already!" he said, pushing his Reader toward mine as I pulled it away again.

"You'll have time. It's short. But first I need to say something, and you need to take it to heart. Everything depends upon it."

I held the device out of his reach. "And I mean everything."

Alexandra walked up to us and interjected "What? He needs to take to heart that he's wasting everyone's time?" Kate shot Alex a look and she sat down with an audible huff.

"Always a joy to hear your sweet voice and nuanced arguments, dear," Hernandez said, without looking toward his daughter.

Everyone except Alexandra stared at me. Even Randy had put aside his computer and was looking at us from the rear of the plane. I felt like I was back at the university, leading a graduate seminar: "Ok, now listen. Dick, you played baseball in college, right?"

"What the hell does baseball have to do with anything?"

"Shut up and listen. This is important."

He sat up straight. I made a mental note of his reaction to my assertiveness.

"As you know, all baseball games have the same rules: nine innings, three strikes, and so on." I couldn't tell if his stare was of interest or annoyance. Kate's look suggested that she was on my side, but that I better hurry up if I wanted to keep his attention.

"The difference between a losing team and a winning team isn't that they play by different rules, but that they know the rules, and how to exploit them. Some baseball games are won by a spectacular home run, or because of great pitching or fielding."

"Or because of errors made by the losing team," Kate added – her clever way of telling me to speed it up.

"Look. Elections have rules too. And some rules don't change: a great debate is always like a home run; a good ad can change the logic of a contest, like a stolen base. But some political rules…" Hernandez was starting to wiggle.

"Bear with me, Senator."

He put his hands on his lap and Kate placed one of hers on top of his, as if to encourage him to hear me out. She was smiling now.

I continued: "Most Americans know the complicated rules of baseball, but almost no one – including most politicians – really understands the rules of politics. Your typical politician doesn't know how voters decide whom to vote for. Or whether to vote. They think they know, but they're almost always wrong. Even the consultants are usually guessing. The only reason anyone wins elections is because the other side was even more clueless."

I stopped for a moment and was pleased that he didn't take advantage of the pause to contradict me.

"No shit, Einstein. Clinton was so oblivious she lost to the pussy-grabbing, Putin-blowing, shithead, idiot conman."

Kate interjected, speaking slowly: "Because she didn't realize that the rules had changed…"

"Exactly, because unlike baseball, political rules change. A new crisis, a new technology, or a new Zeitgeist means new rules. And the politician that sees and understands those changes first has the advantage."

Even Alexandra was staring at me now.

"Zeitgeist?" Antonio said, waking up. "That anything like a Poltergeist?"

"Shut up and go back to sleep, moron," Hernandez chuckled.

"Look, here's the bottom line: knowing how voters decide is the difference between victory and defeat. We can win because we know the new rules and Cranmore doesn't. Hillary Clinton thought they would vote for her because she was smart and qualified and experienced, and because Trump was such an obvious crook..."

I stopped talking and stared at the Senator as he rubbed his chin and looked up at me thoughtfully.

But it was Kate who spoke first: "Clinton was playing by the old rules. Voters were in too pissy a mood to care about competence or experience. They wanted to throw a collective temper tantrum."

"I believe that's *'isterika'* in Russian?" Hernandez interjected, grinning.

"And the rules have changed again!" By now, Kate was reading my mind: "Cranmore thinks the voters will vote for her, as they did last time, because they want stability, decency, and honesty..." She didn't finish the sentence. She didn't have to.

"But what we know..." Hernandez turned toward me as he spoke... "and Cranmore probably doesn't, is that the rules have changed, because of some switchgrass in Iowa and Missouri!"

Kate jumped out of her seat and put both hands on her husband's shoulders. "Get Cranmore to say the wrong thing..." she looked to the side, searching for the right words, "...you know, the wrong thing about the switchgrass! Before she understands what's going on! Then we can go on the offensive!"

Hernandez smiled and took Kate's hand: "So I get Cranmore to minimize the invasive species danger. Get her to call me...I don't know..."

"...an 'environmental extremist!'" Kate smiled.

"Right!" Hernandez continued, "or an 'eco-alarmist' or something like that! And then when the shit-grass hits the fan, so to speak, I look like a prophet."

"Sound the alarm, Dick!" Kate exclaimed, beaming at me. "Sound the alarm!"

Alexandra looked up from her seat, and for the first time ever, she smiled at me. I smiled back at the next First Daughter as I tapped the Senator's Reader with mine.

***

There were only about a dozen people at Betty Rossi's fundraiser, but if you had ever watched the Oscars, you knew them all. When the Senator saw how small the group was, he leaned toward me and whispered that he would speak informally, rather than read my speech.

"Just remember the three main points," I whispered back, "1) invasive GMOs threaten farmers and the economy; 2) greedy corporations don't care; 3) Dick Hernandez does care – and by protecting the environment he will protect the farmers and the economy. Got it, Senator?"

"Got it: Farmers, Greedy Corporations, the Environment, and Me." He smiled the famous Hernandez smile as he entered the room and the actors and directors circled around him.

Betty put her hands up and gave a mercifully brief introduction:

"Hey everyone. As you all know, I supported Sally Cranmore four years ago, and we all credit her for helping to heal the nation's wounds. But I'm hosting this fundraiser for Dick Hernandez because multiple environmental crises threaten our planet, and they won't be stopped by decency alone. There is only one candidate who has the vision we need to build a sustainable economy. As the Senator put it in that wonderful speech he gave yesterday at the Grand Canyon, 'we are all part of the web of life, and whatever we do to the web, we do to ourselves.' Dick understands this like no other politician today. But you don't need to hear it from me. Let's listen to what our next President has to say."

Hernandez thanked Betty and smiled warmly as he patiently gazed around the room. He set his drink on the fireplace mantle.

"My chief speechwriter, Marco Vannicelli…" to my surprise he began by mentioning me… "wrote a terrific speech for me today, but I'm not going to give it, because I know I don't need Marco's beautiful words to move the hearts of *this* committed group of environmentalists. Rather, I want to talk to you, my friends, my *comrades-in-arms*, about why I believe this election is our last chance to stop the climate crisis and other threats to our planet."

He smiled that wonderful smile that said "we're in this together, my dear friend" to each person as he made individual eye contact.

This guy just got better and better at it, didn't he?

Chapter Twelve

I watched the clouds pass beneath us and imagined rain pelting the Great Plains. The twin engines of the 20-seat jet hummed, beckoning me to take a nap, but as I pulled down my window blind, I saw Hernandez approaching. The prosecco bottle in his right hand, and the crystal flutes splayed through the fingers of his left told me there would be no napping in my immediate future. I pushed the window back up.

He was smiling the big Hernandez smile, no doubt because the Rossi fundraiser had gone well. He looked like he was going to propose a toast as he passed several rows of plush tan seats.

But as he placed several glasses on the cushion next to mine and poured bubbly into the one flute remaining in his hand, I noticed there was something wrong with his smile. It didn't reach his eyes.

He shoved the glass over my head toward Antonio on the side sofa. "Hey Tonino!" Their eyes locked.

A gust jolted the plane, knocking the Senator against my seat. Sparkling wine splashed onto my arm, where it fizzled and dripped off as I reached to steady him. Antonio grabbed the glass and held it on the side table until the jet stabilized. Hernandez took a second flute and filled it, as if nothing had happened. He scarcely broke eye contact with Antonio.

"I saw you chatting with some actors, Tonino," the Senator said, leaning against the back of my seat. He handed me the glass, with his eyes still glued to Antonio.

"We were discussing your GMO policy, Senator." Antonio shifted in his seat, but his gaze remained steady. "And the name's Antonio. Sir." Hernandez lifted another flute and filled it for himself.

"You were discussing invasive switchgrass."

Antonio shifted again, so that now he was facing the boss directly. "They all agreed that we need stricter research protocols."

Hernandez held his gaze for several seconds. "A toast!" he said as he raised his glass. I tilted mine reluctantly – I could feel the sarcasm coming. "To stupidity!"

Antonio lifted his glass slightly and shifted again in his seat, so that he was no longer facing the Senator directly. He put it down without taking a sip. His boss leaned over him, placing his free hand on the sofa arm: "Have you read Sun Tzu? *The Art of War*?" Before Antonio could respond, Hernandez shook his head, "What do you think a military strategist might say about the element of surprise?"

He turned and started away, but then spun around and leaned over him again, breathing into his face: "Our only advantage – the one thing we have going for us, you idiot – is we know something Cranmore doesn't! What the hell were you thinking?"

Kate jumped up and grabbed her husband's arm, pointing him toward the back of the plane as she relieved him of the bottle. "Randy wants to show you some poll results!" She shot me a look and tilted her head.

I took her cue. "That's right, Senator." I said as I stood, trying to smile but thinking he really could try to be less of an asshole sometimes. "Shall we go over the numbers?" I grabbed the elbow of his other arm.

Hernandez shook off my hand, spilling prosecco on the floor. Kate held on tight to his other arm, but he spun back toward Antonio, occasioning an arc of liquid that splashed all three of us.

"You should sue your brains for non-support! Tonino!" he spit out as he seized the remaining empty flutes from the seat. I couldn't tell if it was prosecco or saliva, but something wet had hit Antonio's shirt.

"You know something Senator?" Antonio attempted to wipe his shirt clean with a napkin but succeeded only in spreading the senatorial fluid around. "When I look into your eyes, I think I see a sad little boy whose mommy didn't praise him enough."

Hernandez paused. His eyes shifted and he clenched his jaw in what I thought might be a rare moment of self-doubt. No such luck.

"And when I look into your eyes, Dumbo, I see the back of your head!"

"Randy has something to show you!" Kate pulled her husband away from Antonio and dragged him down the aisle. I assisted by pushing from behind.

Randy, seated in the back row, looked up from his computer. He had mustard on his white shirt, and there was a half-eaten sandwich on the seat next to him.

"Show Dick the poll!" Kate begged. She ran her arm through the Senator's and pinned it against her, so he wouldn't be able to turn around again without knocking her over.

"Oh. Right. The poll! Um. I'm still working on the crosstabs, but it looks like support for Cranmore among Democratic voters is broad…"

"Like her hips?" he smirked, his mood shifting back to his default sophomoric, thanks to Kate's distraction.

Randy looked at him blankly. "Broad, but soft, sir."

"As I said."

Randy continued: "Ninety percent of registered Democrats say they expect Cranmore to be the nominee, and 96% say they will vote for her against Canterbury…"

"Did you know Jack Canterbury was the first in his family born without a tail?" Hernandez somehow slipped from Kate's arm, regaining control of the prosecco. He filled another flute and handed it to her. She passed it to Randy.

"A tail, sir?" he said as he took the glass from Kate.

"How many voters said they would like to see another Democrat in the race, Randy?" Kate took the bottle and handed it to me. I placed it on the floor.

"Only 19% of likely Democratic primary voters say they *want* to see another Democrat in the race, but 40% say they *would consider voting* for another Democrat."

"Wow!" Hernandez put down his glass and rubbed his hands together. "So, if all goes well, I might lose by only twenty points! You just made my day, Joseph!"

"Joseph?" Randy said.

"That's your name, right?" Randy stared at him.

"You know, Joseph, when I look into your eyes..."

"Why are you calling me Joseph?"

"Randy has done a great job with this poll." Kate took over, scrutinizing her husband's face. "It shows which Democratic voters are open to an alternative candidate..."

"The most interesting result I see here..." Randy broke back in, "...is that every demographic says Cranmore isn't doing enough on several environmental issues..."

Hernandez was silent as he pushed the half-eaten sandwich onto the floor, sat down next to Randy and looked at the screen. Randy pointed.

"You see here?" When asked whether she's done 'not enough,' 'too much,' or 'about the right amount' on the climate crisis, 80% of Dems say 'not enough.' On the green flies, 91% say she needs to do more. And while most voters can't describe what GMOs are, when invasive organisms are explained to them, 95% support stronger global research protocols!"

Randy turned to Hernandez, smiled, and took a sip of his prosecco.

"She's vulnerable on the environment, sir."

***

The sky was cloudless above as Kate and I huddled at the back of the plane, composing talking points for the Senator to use at the press conference. Randy and Antonio were napping across the aisle. Randy appeared to be in a REM sleep, mumbling something about standard deviations and multiple regressions.

"How is it that you know so much about gene mutation, Kate?" I asked.

"Oh, I guess I have a *New York Times* level understanding. It's common knowledge since CRISPR that we can modify multiple genes in a cell line simultaneously."

"Common knowledge? Most people can't *spell* DNA, my friend."

The cabin darkened slightly, as the plane cut downward through some clouds. "Let's get this to him and make sure he understands how this works," she said. "We'll be landing soon."

"I'll go over the psychology stuff. You explain the technology and keep him focused."

"Everything is riding on this switchgrass thing, Marco, and your idea on how to drag Cranmore into it is brilliant. Absolutely brilliant!"

I grinned. "We make a great team." I watched the shadows of clouds stroll across her thick brown hair.

"We do. And…" She leaned toward me and put her hand on my shoulder, her green eyes moist. "Marco, we both know what an arsehole Dick can be. Childish – and mean when he's worried. But he's so talented. And he really does care. It's not just politics. I know you can see that too."

She studied my face for signs of dissent that I managed not to show. "And he just might be the world's last, best hope. It was 40 goddamn degrees Celsius in Helsinki last week!"

Alexandra came back, sat next to her mother, and smiled at me for the second time. Her eyes weren't bloodshot, and she didn't smell like pot.

"Mom's right. He's a total dick sometimes, but that dick just might save the world. Not bad for an eight-year-old in a man's body, huh?" For the first time, I noticed she had her mother's smile and green eyes.

"Let's school him on GMOs," I said, standing. Kate got up, but Alexandra remained seated. I looked at her.

"Aren't you coming?" I heard myself say. "I'm sure Dad can use his newest fan's help with his homework!"

***

The plane door opened. The odor of melting tar filled my nostrils and my watch's heat alarm went off. A cloud of green flies approached like a welcoming committee. Hernandez looked at them and smiled. The press strolled out of the terminal toward a platform set up with microphones. There were more journalists than I had expected, and most wore Cool-Fans on their collars. One sported one of those new SolarCool-Hats – it fluffed her white linen suit, and she looked so comfortable that I made a mental note to see what they cost.

As we walked slowly across the tarmac, brushing the flies away, I reminded Hernandez to emphasize emotional appeals. "Grab them first, Senator. Flatter them. Get them to *want* to believe you. Only then will they listen to evidence and arguments. And stress what an underdog you are – journalists love a David and Goliath story."

"After you have them, go after Cranmore!" Kate said.

"She's Goliath, right?" He was looking ahead and grinning for any cameras that might be on us.

Kate stared ahead. "Just trying to keep you on message, dear. This is the moment! Do this right, and when you step away from those microphones, millions of Democratic voters will be wondering why the President has been asleep at the wheel. While invasive organisms like these flies…"

"Hey!" he smirked, "maybe I should ask some flies to join me up there and say a few words. You know, buzzwords?"

"Jesus, Dick! Get serious!" She patted her forehead with a handkerchief. "Make Cranmore defend her do-nothing record. Get her to take the bait!"

"Remember," I added, "walk that line between being your usual loveable self and getting a bit hot under the collar. We want Cranmore to say you're overreacting. The more she tries to minimize what you say, the better."

Alexandra came up behind us and whispered in his ear:

"If you get this right, Daddy, I'll never call you 'Senator Fucking Loser Douchebag' again."

Hernandez winked at her before stepping to the microphones. He looked at the journalists gathered before him and smiled the magic smile. His eyes shined. He had never been more ready.

Chapter Thirteen

Hernandez climbed the steps to the platform as I slipped behind the crowd to observe his body language from where the journalists stood. He placed one hand on the lectern and, with a handkerchief in his other hand, dabbed his forehead. Waves of heat rose off the tarmac and upwards toward the cruel sun. A breeze bore the stink of melting tar, but it was too weak to stop the Mexican flies buzzing around everyone's heads. Several journalists had turned their Cool-Fans upon the invasive pests, as if battery-operated personal fans could somehow push away the consequences of our collective folly.

The Senator looked relaxed and in control, smiling beatifically. He surveyed the journalists, stopping on each face and lighting up his eyes, as if to express delight at seeing each one, before moving on to the next. His gaze met mine and we both nodded. Kate and Alexandra were below, off-stage in the shade, sharing a Cool-Fan and holding hands, looking up at him. Kate's brow was furrowed, but when Alexandra whispered something in her ear, her face muscles relaxed.

Hernandez leaned toward the microphones, brushed his black hair off his brow, and looked at the cameras: "Hey, thanks for coming everyone! It's hot, so I won't keep you for long."

"Must be even hotter for you in that suit, Senator," the woman with the SolarCool-Hat and white linen suit called out. I couldn't tell if she was being kind or not, but Hernandez gave her the benefit of the doubt:

"I'm fine thanks, Chang Ying." His talent for remembering faces and names was extraordinary. "Just trying to reduce my carbon footprint. It was supposed to be only 90 degrees this week, so I left my Cool-Fan at home. I grew up in Southern California, so I'm pretty resilient. It was hot there before hot was cool."

Some of the journalists chuckled at his double entendre, but one man shouted out a challenge: "Couldn't help noticing you arrived by private jet, Senator. Is that how you reduce your carbon footprint? Shouldn't the 'environmentalist candidate' set a better example?"

Fearing that question, I had urged him not to schedule the news conference on the tarmac, but he had laughed at me. So now, with that goddamn old-style jet-engine plane behind him in all its carbon-churning glory, he would have to explain himself. I hoped he would wiggle out of it by saying something meaningless but distracting, like "the plane's owner is a carbon-neutral flyer," and then pivoting to his climate policy before he got a follow-up question.

"Glad you asked, Juan," Hernandez turned and pointed at the plane, smiling as he informed them that the moon was made of green cheese: "That's a carbon-neutral plane, with solar-charged batteries!"

What the hell was he saying?! I considered how I might clean this one up as "Juan" pointed at the twin jet engines. But before the journalist could say anything, the Senator added: "It's a beautiful thing – a carbon-neutral plane." And then, with a twinkle in his eye, he pointed directly at me. "My Chief Energy Advisor, Mr. Vannicelli, will explain in a moment how it works."

As the crowd turned toward me, I smiled and nodded confidently, without a clue as to what I was going to say. Should I try to maintain his "solar plane" bullshit? I quickly discarded this option, as we were sure to get caught. Maybe I should walk the statement back, explaining that what he meant was that the owner of the plane purchased carbon credits at 100%? There was a reasonable chance that this was true, but what if it wasn't? I decided my best option was to slip away when no one was looking, hoping they would forget about me.

Hernandez pivoted, both physically and rhetorically as he leaned forward: "But before I hand you over to Mr. Vannicelli, I want to discuss an environmental problem that hasn't been getting enough attention. As you know, Juan, for years scientists warned us about climate change, but we ignored them. And now we're facing the staggering costs of that historic failure to act on time. Sea levels have risen dramatically, driving millions from their homes around the world. Forests burn, crops fail, massive storms destroy entire cities. Antarctica – well, we all know what happened there! Coral reefs, glaciers and once-productive fisheries are gone forever. Because we failed to act on climate change – and now we race to adapt to a global crisis that we could have, and should have, prevented."

As if to drive his point home, he took out his handkerchief and wiped his brow again.

"I've introduced new 'carbon-negative' legislation in the Senate, and I have called on President Cranmore to support it and to re-start the 'Global Zero Now' negotiations."

Hernandez paused and shook his head like a disappointed parent.

"So far, I am sad to say, she has done neither of these things." He paused again, still shaking his head slowly.

"I don't understand what she's waiting for."

He paused a third time, brushed some flies from his face, and looked straight into the cameras:

"So much is at stake, President Cranmore. So much. Where are you? Why won't you lead?" His direct challenge to the President worked perfectly. Rhetorically, he had made her personally responsible for the climate crisis.

He stopped again, letting it all sink in as he looked at each journalist individually. Again, the handkerchief came out and across his brow.

"And, Madam President," he continued, raising his voice slightly. "When are you going to face up to the other, urgent, environmental problem that scientists have been warning us about? Are you going to continue to ignore that problem too? Until it's too late – again?"

He had them in the palm of his hand, wondering what that other problem was. He kept them waiting a few seconds before letting them know:

"I'm talking about the danger to our ecosystems – and to our economy – posed by invasive, genetically modified organisms. These flies buzzing around our heads have migrated north from Central America because of climate change. They're annoying, but there are other, far more dangerous organisms that could do truly enormous damage." He paused to deafening silence. "And as we speak, such organisms are being developed in laboratories around the world."

Some of the journalists looked confused, but he pulled them back by raising both his hand and his voice: "President Cranmore!" He said it loud, pointing upward at nothing in particular, but it made a great image. "Please, President Cranmore – we must not miss the boat again!"

Hernandez stopped to again make eye contact with the journalists.

"The President, my friends, is sleepwalking toward another avoidable environmental calamity. Around the world, GMO research is taking place with only the weakest of safeguards to keep new organisms in the lab until we are sure they pose no threat. This is unacceptable. Because once an organism gets out into the wild and starts reproducing, that's it. No matter how destructive a new plant or animal might be, once it's out there, it stays out there. It's a genie that you cannot put back in the bottle."

He paused and leaned forward, turning a microphone toward his face:

"I am calling on President Cranmore to seek, immediately, a comprehensive global accord on GMO research!" He paused, "And if she isn't willing to do so, she needs to explain to the American people exactly why not. Does the President think scientists are making this up? Is she going to deny the danger, as so many politicians denied the danger of climate change? Why does she think we should keep playing Russian Roulette with GMOs?"

He stared at the journalists and issued his challenge: "Tell us, President Cranmore, do we need new global research controls or not? If not, tell us why not! If so, why are you not leading on this? Where are you? Why are you not doing your job?"

By now the journalists had forgotten all about me and the airplane. As they began to pepper Hernandez with questions, I ducked into the terminal. The blast of cool air at first was refreshing, but soon my sweaty shirt felt cold and clammy on my skin. I sat down in a bar by the gate, where I could see the Senator through a window. He stood erect and confident, pointing at journalists, one by one, as they asked questions.

A pleasant waiter with a short afro took my order. When he returned with my beer, the young man tilted his head toward the window and asked if I was with "that guy speaking outside." I told him I was.

"He's a Senator, right? That guy who really knows his shit, right? What's his name?"

"Hernandez. Dick Hernandez. Good guy," I said.

"About time!"

"About time for what?"

"About time someone took all this seriously. I'm 24 years old. I need this planet to last another 70 years or so!"

"Smart kid," I thought, grateful that I wouldn't be around in 70 years. I asked him: "So you heard what the Senator was saying?"

"Sure did. He's got my vote," he said as he walked toward the next table to take an order. "Got my vote."

I considered how Hernandez had turned his dumb comment about the plane to his advantage. He had pivoted to the climate crisis and then pushed every button he needed to win over those journalists. The media now would take the GMO issue to Cranmore, who would have no choice but to respond to his challenge. Either she would support his call to action – and it would look like he was leading and she was following – or she would have to explain why she thought he was exaggerating the threat of GMOs. Either way, we would have her playing defense.

I looked out the window and up at white cumulous clouds far above Hernandez, moving toward us and starting to cast a shadow over him and the journalists. My mind drifted with the clouds. I remembered when I was five or six and I had fallen off my bike after trying to go too fast down a hill. I lay on the ground, looking to the sky and crying as my mother caressed my forehead and kissed my scratches. She picked me up, held me to her chest and said something that, at that age, I couldn't have understood: *"Non tutto il male viene per nuocere, piccolino,"* she had said, "not all bad things do harm, little one."

She smiled as she repeated it, kissing me on the cheek. "Someday, you'll understand, Marcolino," she said, whispering it into my ear: *"Non tutto il male viene per nuocere."*

Chapter Fourteen

Humid air stole through the window of the Senate office, carrying the smell of cut grass and the hum of a lawn turtle. My watch said it was 8:00 PM and 94 F degrees, but it felt later and hotter. The remains of an old-style electric air conditioner, its use now illegal, lay on the floor behind the Senator, covered by a frayed curtain and some orphaned filing boxes.

Hernandez and I were alone – his staff had gone for the day, and the campaign team had gone out for Chinese food. I wiped my forehead with the back of my hand, walked to the window, and pulled it down, unsure of whether it was the humidity or the lawn turtle that was annoying me. Or whether it was something else altogether. With the window closed, the only sounds left were of a vacuum-bot somewhere down the hallway, bumping repeatedly and senselessly against a wall, and the ticking of the Senator's Reader as he page-winked through the material I had texted him.

"They better not forget the hot and sour soup," he said, more to himself than to me. His tie lay on the floor beside him, and his phone was perched on the rim of the desk, inches from his elbow. It began to call out Kate's name and vibrate toward the edge. He grabbed it without looking up from his reading.

"Don't forget the hot and sour soup," he said, punching the speaker icon. "You want anything else?" He looked at me over the top of his Reader, but before I could answer Kate said they were already on their way back.

"How you can eat hot soup on a day like today is beyond me. Just wanted to remind you to turn on Fox," she said.

"Hurry up, would you? I'm getting sick of listening to Vannicelli's stomach growling. I think he must have a live wolverine in there." I was impressed by this expression, however backhanded, of concern. Baby steps, Dicky, I thought. Baby steps.

"The Lester Downs interview starts in five minutes," Kate reminded him. "I want to hear it live. Turn it on!" I could tell from her breathing that she was already climbing the Capitol stairs.

"I don't have time for Downs. Just tell me if Cranmore says anything interesting to that miserable, lying creep."

"You wouldn't be suggesting Downs is a dishonest, slimy, double-talking, opportunistic sleazebag, would you?" I heard her say.

"Good point, love," he conceded with a short chuckle. "Some of my favorite colleagues are miserable, lying creeps."

"And that would be a bad thing, right? Turn it on – Cranmore might say something about you."

"I doubt it. She knows the best way to deal with a longshot challenger is to ignore him."

Kate hung up without saying goodbye – her way of letting her husband know what to do. "Turn on Lester Downs," he commanded the office bot, without looking up from his reading. President Cranmore instantly appeared on the wall-screen, looking comfortable and confident as she strode onto the set, took Downs' hand, and smiled warmly at a man she surely loathed. The Veri-Monitor was flashing red across the chyron: "Low Veri-rated Programming – Real-time Fact-check Auto-active."

"Lower Volume," Hernandez said, and the bot obliged. He turned toward me: "You know how you can tell when Downs is lying, Joseph?"

I pretended to ignore him.

"You know how you can tell when that lowlife is lying, Joseph?"

"No one here by that name, Senator."

"The same way you can tell if Cranmore is thinking. She moves her lips."

"Hilarious."

"Where's my fucking hot and sour soup?"

Alexandra came through the door, turned her gaze to the monitor and sat next to her father, placing two bags in front of him on the desk. The Chinese food smelled greasy but good. Kate entered and sat on Dick's other side. All three regarded the screen.

"Volume Up!" Kate instructed and the bot obeyed. "She's about to put her foot in her mouth. I can sense it!"

"Hope she has a size 11 mouth," Dick smirked as he put down the Reader and began unpacking the Chinese food. He looked torn between the eggrolls and the President, who was now seated and grinning. Downs spoke first:

"Thank you for this opportunity, President Cranmore, to discuss your reelection campaign. As you know, your rival, Senator Hernandez…" Cranmore's eyes turned cold.

"…says you aren't doing enough to stop American companies from developing better food crops. He says these job-creating businesses are going to unleash some sort of plague or something. The Senator from California claims that genetically modified crops are dangerous to the environment. Surely you don't agree with all this scaremongering?"

Kate and Alexandra exchanged glances. Hernandez, who had been moving an eggroll toward his face, put it down and rubbed greasy fingers across his chin as he stared at the screen. I grabbed an eggroll quickly and shoved it into my mouth. Pungent mustard fumes filled my nostrils as I scrutinized Cranmore's face smiling implausibly at Downs.

"Hey look! She's thinking without moving her lips!" Hernandez snickered, as he reached again for his eggroll.

But before Cranmore could answer the question, the Fox propagandist asked another:

"Do you think, Madam President, that Dick Hernandez even knows what he's saying? I mean, he talks a good game, but I wonder if he's just another greenie who doesn't get that technology is what makes America great. What do you think,

Madam President? Is Hernandez as smart as he thinks he is? Invasive GMOs? C'mon. I mean, really?"

Her answer started off as a classic Cranmore straddle – something for everyone: "Well, Lester, you know the issue of genetically modified organisms is complex, and we have scientists studying whether they pose any dangers. Clearly, we need to protect our environment, while also boosting food production, and developing therapies for terrible diseases. You know, there's no evidence that GMO foods are a health risk…"

The Veri-Monitor flashed yellow: "True, but Misleading – question was not about food risks."

Hernandez shoved the eggroll into his mouth. "This is why she'll never be on Mount Rushmore," he said as he chewed. "She has too many faces."

"But," Downs continued, "hasn't science shown that there are no dangers from GMOs? Isn't this more hysterical eco-nonsense, motivated by Senator Hernandez' well-known hatred for successful people?"

Cranmore hesitated. Kate and Alexandra wiggled in their seats. Dick was trying to remove the cover from the soup container, but he couldn't take his eyes off the screen. The lid resisted his efforts by spinning, rather than popping off.

"Well Lester. I believe that a President must be a good steward of the environment…"

Kate and Alexandra leaned together toward the monitor.

"But Senator Hernandez, well, he's a good Senator, and a friend of mine…"

"Right. That's why I quit her do-nothing administration!" Hernandez grumbled, struggling with the soup, trying to get his large fingers under the lid.

"But let's be frank, Lester, when it comes to the environment, the Senator is a bit prone to exaggeration."

Alexandra jumped out of her seat. "Did she really say that?"

"Is she truly so stupid?" Kate said, following Alexandra up and putting her arm around her daughter's shoulder as they stared at the screen.

"I think she's been possessed by a retarded demon." Hernandez laughed as he pressed forcefully on both sides of the soup container.

Mother and daughter started shaking fists in the air, the way bettors urge their ponies around the final stretch.

Cranmore hesitated, and then she said what we had been hoping for: "You know, Lester, Senator Hernandez can be a bit of an environmental alarmist!"

A geyser of hot and sour soup shot up out of the container and hit Hernandez in the face. As it dripped off his nose, Kate hugged him and Alexandra clasped them both from behind. Soup dripped over them all as they laughed with delight.

"She said it, Dick! She said it!" Kate cried, kissing his wet cheek and rubbing soup into his hair with both hands. "That shithead Downs actually got her to say it!"

"No more 'Senator Fucking Loser Douchebag' for you, Daddy!" Alexandra beamed. "From now on, you're 'The Fucking Environmental Alarmist!'"

"And next year, Senator," I said as I walked over to him and extended my hand, "with a few more lucky breaks like this, you're going to be 'The Fucking Environmental President!'"

PART THREE

The worst of all deceptions is self-deception.

— Plato

The waiter placed a glass of Barbera on the table. I held it to the light, hoping the dance of purple reflexes might distract me from the knot in my stomach.

Why had I called her? What could either of us have to say? I put the glass down and started toward the exit. I'd tell her something had come up. I'd think of something.

"Marco! I thought I was early!" She stepped through the door and strode past the Maître D', toward me. The floral dress she wore looked familiar.

"Such a nice surprise to hear from you!" She smiled as she took my hands; I felt the warmth of hers. "So, the President's Svengali actually has time to invite an old friend to lunch?"

I pulled away and tilted my head, but I didn't let go. "Svengali? You see me as a hypnotist?" The comparison bothered me.

She chuckled, swaying her arms and squeezing my hands, which had the effect of pulling me gently toward her. I smelled a familiar scent.

"Marco, I've known you a long time. We were kids together! I know that behind that cynical façade there's a mensch…" She paused, "… and someone who, though he might deny it, cares about what's true."

I looked into her brown eyes and recalled them filled with tears. She lowered her voice, whispering: "You're no Svengali. But don't worry – your secret's safe with me. And I'm glad you had time for lunch!"

Over her shoulder, through a window, I could see in the distance a corner of the White House. I noticed that the knot in my stomach was gone, and that an unfamiliar sensation had come over me: I felt lighter, looser, more comfortable – as if I had shed a skin I no longer needed.

"I've all the time in the world now. Returned my credentials an hour ago." I glanced at her phone. "It's probably out there already, if you want to check the news." Her eyes remained locked on mine.

"You've given up on Hernandez?"

"Not exactly. He's doing his best. It's just…"

A waiter glanced at us as he walked by, wondering why we were standing.

"Is this our table?" she asked. I nodded and we sat.

"Any plans?" She leaned toward me. "I mean, now that you'll have time for a life?" She pointed at my glass. "You going to drink that alone?" I waved to the waiter, circling my hand first at the wine, and then toward Mary.

"It's great to see you. What's it been? Two years? The last time, I was giving some silly conference paper…"

I relaxed back in my chair. "Too long. Too long," I heard myself say. "It's wonderful to see you too." I wasn't being polite. I was glad she was there.

"Marco." She leaned toward me. "There's something I want to share with you. Something I've wanted to tell you for a very long time." She paused before pinching her shoulders. "Remember this dress?"

The waiter placed a glass of wine in front of her. She lifted it to eye level.

"Barbera d'Asti, right?"

Chapter Fifteen

We sat around the office conference table, Hernandez and Kate on one side, Randy and I at opposite ends. It was getting dark outside, and we had dimmed the lights so as not to attract green flies through the open window. The sound was off on the wall monitor, but the image of a CNN journalist and a farmer walking through fields of stunted corn told the story.

"Look Senator," Randy raised his hands as if he was holding something out for him to see. "My polling shows that 70% of voters can't tell you what an invasive GMO is. Hell, even those who can don't see why they should care."

"Right." Hernandez' smirk told me more was coming: "So you've discovered that most voters aren't geneticists or ecologists, have you Randy? What else is new?"

The farmer on CNN peeled open a corn cob, revealing small black specks where there should have been big yellow kernels.

"What I'm saying, Senator, is that this GMO thing doesn't have the legs politically we hoped it might. You'd have to educate people about what genetically modified organisms are, and why invasive species are threatening. It's too complicated – you're trying to scare them about something they don't understand. It won't work…"

"Nonsense, Randy!" I interrupted. "Just the opposite. It'll work precisely because people don't understand it!"

"There's nothing more terrifying than the unknown," Kate was looking at Randy, but speaking to her husband, as she backed me up. "Think about it – most people can't explain how carbon pollution damages the climate. But they know that it does. When they see climate refugee camps in Sicily, ice storms in Florida, or a tornado tearing through the Upper West Side, they don't understand the climate science. But they don't have to – they can see that something has gone wrong. And not understanding exactly WHAT has gone wrong, makes it all the scarier!"

Hernandez was shaking his head and looking at the monitor. He looked…sad. Kate placed a hand on his shoulder. "Voters don't have to know WHY the GMO switchgrass is a threat. They only need to see fields of corn and soy that don't grow anymore."

"And farmers despairing because they can't pay their bills," I added. "This is political dynamite. And it's real. It's hurting people. Farmers today, consumers tomorrow."

Hernandez rubbed his chin. "It's just goddamn awful what's happening. Look at that poor guy!" He pointed to the farmer on the screen. "He gets up every morning and does what he's always done. Plays by the rules. But nothing works – his corn doesn't grow. Because it's being suffocated by weeds!" He seemed genuinely concerned about the farmer. "Why does he have to go out of business? What the hell did he do?"

Kate nodded, placing her hand on her husband's shoulder and looking into his yes. "Let's win this election for that guy, Dick!"

Randy took his laptop into the next room and started pecking at his keyboard. Kate and the Senator turned toward me, but before I could speak, Alexandra stepped in and looked at the monitor.

"Even Fox is reporting it, you naughty alarmist, you!" she said, grinning at her father. "Cranmore seems to have gone into hiding. And we just got a call from guess who?"

"WHO?" all three of us asked simultaneously.

"I'll give you a hint." Her eyes sparkled. "He's the biggest fraud in American journalism."

***

"A pleasure to have you on the show, Senator." Lester Downs smiled at Hernandez with the sincerity of a pickpocket. We were expecting a rough interview – Antonio had been working the Capitol Hill bars, and the scuttlebutt was that Canterbury wanted us out of the race, so he could run against "Do-Nothing Cranmore." Fox was going to be tough on us.

"So glad you were able to take some time out of your busy schedule terrifying the American public, Senator…"

Hernandez interrupted politely but quickly: "The last thing I want to do is terrify people, Lester. We're faced with an invasive species crisis, and President Cranmore needs to take action now, before it's too late."

"Excellent!" I said to Kate, who was perched on the edge of the office couch next to me, staring intently at the screen. "He's not letting Downs frame the discussion!" She waved her hand in my direction to hush me.

He continued: "But thanks for inviting me on the show, so I can explain why this problem is so urgent. Crops are failing across the Midwest…"

"Oh, come on, Senator. Are you really going to lose your cool over a little switchgrass? Weeds are just part of farming, aren't they? As they always have been? Maybe these crops just need some rain. You environmentalists panic every time Mother Nature…"

"Lester…" He smiled the trademark Hernandez smile and spoke clearly but calmly as he interrupted Downs again: "Mother Nature has nothing to do with this. Mother Nature gives us sun and soil and water and life – not herbicide-resistant GMO switchgrass that makes it impossible for farmers to grow their crops."

"But don't you remember…"

"I'll tell you what I remember. I remember climate change deniers," he paused for emphasis, "like you Lester," he paused again, "telling us that global warming wasn't real. Claiming, without evidence, that the scientists were wrong. I remember corporate apologists telling us their plastics and pesticides weren't hormone disruptors." He leaned in and faced the camera. "And today there are tropical fish

in Lake Michigan, and three-eyed male trout with ovaries in the Missouri river!
Three. Eyed. Trout."

Hernandez stopped to let the image of mutant trout sink in, before delivering
the *coup de grace*: "We aren't talking about Mother Nature. Because nothing about
this is natural. There's nothing natural about three-eyed trout, and there's nothing
natural about genetically modified weeds suffocating crops and ruining our farmers."

Lester Downs leaned back momentarily, but then sat up, trying to take the
offensive. "Well, leaving aside the climate change controversy..."

"There's no controversy." Hernandez was still smiling, and clearly in control
of the interview. "There's a climate crisis. What there isn't anymore is a Glacier
National Park in Montana – because the glaciers are gone. What there isn't is a
Great Coral Reef – because there's no more coral. What there isn't is a skiing industry anywhere in the USA, or any lobsters in Maine – or anymore of just about
anything except jellyfish in the Gulf of Mexico."

He turned toward the camera and spoke directly into it: "And now, people like
you are denying still another crisis. I won't have that. People need to know what's
going on, even if you and President Cranmore don't want to tell them."

Kate and Alexandra grinned as Hernandez skillfully linked Cranmore to
rightwing media.

"Call me an alarmist if you wish," he continued, "but I intend to sound the
alarm until the President acts to help our farmers, who are losing their livelihoods
as invasive switchgrass spreads through their fields. They've already lost rye and
barley to climate change. If they also lose corn and soy – because of herbicide-
resistant GMO switchgrass – our hardworking farmers will be out of business!"

Downs ignored the substance of what he had said, of course, and went personal:
"So that's what this is about? The Midwest primaries, right? You think farmers are
gullible enough to fall for your unsubstantiated claims that somehow switchgrass
is a threat to corn? What's next? Are you going to tell us that wild pigs are going
to eat all our fruits and vegetables? Not everyone is as *educated* as you, Senator, but
just how stupid do you think farmers are?"

Hernandez smiled benignly as he let Downs' ill-chosen words hang in the air. The Fox host squirmed a bit and cleared his throat, hoping that Hernandez would speak, but he said nothing, knowing that this silence was, for him, golden.

Finally, Downs spoke: "Senator, you say you are here to sound the alarm. So, President Cranmore was right when she called you an 'environmental alarmist?'"

Hernandez delivered the words we had prepared to turn the President and the rightwing journalist into kissing cousins: "Mr. Downs," he said, switching to a more formal tone to add gravitas to what would come next: "You and some others may see me as an environmental alarmist…"

"The President called you that. Those were Sally Cranmore's words, not mine!"

Alexandra, Kate and I jumped out of our chairs – Downs' attempt to counter Dick's tactic had instead handed him an even bigger club to beat his rival with:

"Well, it's good to see that you, Lester, might be coming around, albeit belatedly, to recognizing that our planet isn't something we can exploit and mistreat endlessly without regard for the consequences. I'm heartened to see that even a climate science denier like you isn't willing to embrace President Cranmore's even more extreme denialism about the risks of unregulated GMOs."

Hernandez then paused before adding, "I don't care what the President's corporate donors want. Whether it's switchgrass, whether it's pigs, GMOs need to be regulated better. To protect the American people."

Alexandra squinted, tilted her head, and mouthed the word: "PIGS?" Kate, her eyes glued to the monitor, raised a victory fist.

Downs' eyes darted from side to side. Hernandez continued: "The fact that even you can't bring yourself to defend President Cranmore's environmental record shows just how detached from reality she is."

He stopped himself, leaving his last words for millions of viewers to consider. He knew what would be next:

"Well, it looks like we have to go to a …" Before Downs could get the words "commercial break" out of his mouth, Hernandez looked into the camera and drove his message home:

"Thanks for giving me this opportunity to speak to – and for – the farmers and citizens of this country that President Cranmore doesn't see, doesn't hear, and doesn't seem to care about. The good folks who think the time for denial and deflection is over, and that the time for action is..."

A commercial for Eco-Beef, featuring a smiling cartoon cow, came on: "Mooooove over, climate-busting livestock..."

"Monitor off!" I said, and the screen went dark. "We need to do a press release! What's the name of that English scientist that's always on CNN? The one who knows everything about GMOs? You know, young woman, brown hair. What's her name?"

Kate responded immediately: "Rachel Richards. I'll ring her mobile."

I was surprised she had the scientist's name on the tip of her tongue, and her cellphone number, but I was focused on what we needed to know. "We need to find out if Dick was just winging it again with this thing about pigs."

"Of course. I'll call Rachel and see what she knows about any transgenic pigs."

Alexandra popped open a bottle of Cool-Cola, poured half of it into a glass and took a sip. She looked at me and held up the bottle. "Want some?"

I turned toward Kate, leaving Alexandra with her arm outstretched. "I need to talk to this Rachel person before the journalists start calling to ask about pigs!"

Kate's tone was still polite, but firm. "No problem. I'll ask her about the pigs and let you know what she said."

I'd never seen Kate so rigid – and I needed to get the press release out quickly. I looked at her, perplexed. My back hurt. "What's the problem? Why do you need to talk to her?"

"For a very good reason."

"And what would that be? What's the goddam problem?"

"What did I just tell you her name is?"

"'Rachel Richards.' So what?" I leaned against the wall and pressed my thumbs into a knotted muscle along my lumbar spine.

"What's my last name?" She was staring at me. "The goddamn problem, dear friend, is that Rachel Richards is my daughter!"

Silence fell over the office, except for the sound of a glass of Cool-Cola shattering as it hit the floor.

***

I looked across the corner of the Reflecting Pool at Kate and Alexandra, grimacing and gesticulating as they circled each other like prizefighters. They had not seen me following them as Kate ran after her daughter down the Capitol steps and across the Mall.

Alexandra, winded from running, her face contorted with confusion, pleaded for an explanation. I placed both hands on my knees to catch my breath and looked into the water – the face staring back at me held the same perplexed expression. Looking up again, I regarded Alexandra swinging her arms over her head and stamping her feet like a toddler.

A surge of rage at Kate rose up in my chest, as I considered her lifetime of mendacity. But then the rage receded like a tide, leaving only sadness – a sorrow that grew, like a plant reaching for the sun, into empathy. Tears descended my cheeks as I thought how Kate's heart must have ached when little Alexandra, as most only-children do – as I had – begged for a sister or brother.

I watched the dance of the afternoon sun, sparkling across the water's surface, and wondered why they didn't let children swim in the pool. Still out of breath, and feeling lightheaded, I leaned against the marble steps and beheld the little Italian girl in the floral dress jumping and splashing happily in the cool water. I could see her face much clearer than I had in past visions. She had brown eyes and a gentle smile.

Kate reached into her handbag, took out her phone, and stood next to Alexandra so that Rachel could see them both. She spoke for several minutes, holding Alexandra's hand, and then handed the phone to her and kissed her cheek. She looked at me across the water, before leaving her two adult daughters to speak to each other for the first time. As she approached, her eyes were bloodshot, but she appeared relieved.

Kate also looked focused – she had a task to perform. She took my arm and pulled me toward her. I was expecting an explanation, or perhaps a philosophical thought. But instead, incredibly, she got right down to campaign business:

"Listen, he wasn't bullshitting about the pigs. Rachel says there's been another GMO…incident. And this one's a doozy! We need to act fast."

I stared at her. "Really? Is that all you have to say? You just told your daughter you'd been lying to her for twenty years," I gestured toward the pool, "hiding a sister from her?!" I felt again that strange sensation of rage rising and then softening into sorrow, "…and you want to talk to me about pigs?! Really, Kate?"

She squeezed my arm. "It's…complicated. I'll explain later. Right now, we need to focus. The stakes are high, and we don't have much time…"

"You think she's OK?" I nodded toward Alexandra. Kate looked toward her, and her face muscles softened. A tear ran down her cheek.

"She's a smart kid, and wise beyond her years. She'll be pissed at me for a while – and rightfully so – but she'll be OK." Kate pleaded with sad, bloodshot eyes: "Please don't judge me, Marco! This is the moment I have most dreaded – and the moment I have most dreamed of – for twenty years. It's a mind-fuck. A total mind-fuck. I had to tell her sooner or later. There never was a right moment…"

"Are you OK?" I heard myself say.

"I'm fine. I'm glad she was willing to listen. She's taking it better than I had any right to hope…"

"Look, I'm sure you had your reasons…" I heard my own words, as if they came from somewhere outside myself. "I'm sure you had your reasons, my friend."

She interrupted me. "We don't have much time – the press will be showing up any minute now. Our story is that we're looking into reports about GMO pigs. And then we refer them to Rachel – she'll know what to say."

I nodded in agreement. Kate looked into my eyes. "Dick doesn't know about Rachel either…" She paused again. "Randy…" She shook her head, as if she had changed her mind about something. "…It's a long story. I'll tell you later."

A sudden fatigue came over me. I placed my hand on her shoulder to steady myself. She scrutinized my face.

"It's OK," I said. "Just a bit dizzy. Better now." I tried to stand erect and look stronger than I felt. I inhaled deeply and smelled the mist rising from the water.

"Right, then. I'll tell Dick – I have to – but not straightaway. We need to keep him steady until the vote." She glanced over at Alexandra, sitting on the grass next to a "Keep Off The Grass" sign, as she spoke to the sister she never knew. "Oh, and Rachel will be joining the campaign. How could she not at this point?"

"You want me to do anything?" I asked. "I mean, I could warm Dick up? Try to feel him out?"

"You're very kind, my dear friend, but this is something I've been rehearsing for well over twenty years. I know my husband, and I always knew…" she paused, "…I knew this day would come. I was a coward to wait so long, but I know what I need to do – and you know what you need to do! It's only weeks until the first-round primaries, and if we handle this well…Marco?"

Her eyes opened wide as she grabbed me – breaking my fall and guiding me onto the soft grass of the Mall.

Looking up as the world faded to darkness, I saw my mother's face in the clouds.

Chapter Sixteen

"Marco?" I luxuriated in the warmth of my mother's arms, as the hand of a little girl caressed my forehead. Even though my eyes were shut, I knew that they both were smiling lovingly at me. I tried to recall the girl's name.

"Marco? Are you all right?"

Ma cradled my head. I felt safe. There was nowhere else I wanted to be. But why was she speaking English instead of Italian?

"Wake up, Marco! Bloody hell!"

And what's with the English accent? Besides, she's dead!

***

I opened my eyes and smelled the freshly cut grass. Kate was kneeling over me, with Alexandra standing behind her. The distant hum of traffic was soft and unoffensive.

"Been quite a day, hasn't it?" I said, sitting up. The sun emerged from behind a cloud. I squinted.

"Should I call an ambulance?" Alexandra lowered herself to the grass next to me.

I shook my head – Dick had kicked ass in the Lester Downs interview. We didn't want to step on that story.

"I'm OK." The sun felt good on my face. Kate took my right arm and Alexandra my left, helping me to my feet.

"Careful." Kate put her arm around my waist. "You might be shaky."

But I didn't feel shaky at all. I felt strong. Energized.

And I remembered! I remembered the girl in the floral dress. She was a real person!

"You sure you're OK?"

"I feel fine." I looked into Kate's green eyes as the blue sky started to turn soft red at the horizon. "I feel great."

The three of us walked toward the McCain Building, side by side, Kate in the middle. A gentle breeze stroked my forehead. It smelled clean and fresh. The sun was warm, but not hot and, unusually, there were no green flies.

"The air smells good," I said. Kate nodded in agreement. Alexandra, her hand around Kate's waist, rested her head on her mother's shoulder.

"Indeed. Like it used to when we first came to Washington, when Alexandra was little, before the…"

I raised my hand and she stopped speaking – mentioning the deteriorating climate would have broken the spell. As we walked back to the office, I considered how close the three of us had become in recent months. Alexandra and Kate were more than friends. They felt like family.

Family. Something I hadn't experienced in years.

As we entered the office, I whispered in Kate's ear: "I have something to tell you…" I tilted my head toward the back.

A young woman who had been sitting in the waiting area, jumped out of her seat and approached us.

"Katherine Richards?" The woman was petite and thin, but she placed her body in front of us like a goalie. Her straight black hair was stylishly short, and she wore a smart linen suit and diamond stud earrings. "Katherine Richards Hernandez?" Kate looked at the woman with a discernable lack of warmth.

"Kim Yee from Politi-web News," she pushed her phone toward Kate. "Could you comment on the rumor…"

Kate stopped her with a raised hand and a cold smile. "I don't comment on rumors, Ms. Yee. Thank you." She turned away, with the minimum courtesy due an aggressive, uninvited journalist. The woman circled with her, still holding up her phone – this wasn't the first time she had tried to pry a statement out of a public figure.

"Do you have an appointment, Ms. Lee?" I asked, placing myself between them.

"That's 'Yee,' Mr. Vannicelli." She pronounced my name slowly and smiled: "Perhaps the Senator's Senior Everything Advisor might wish to comment on…?"

Kate interrupted: "As I said, we don't…"

"I have a report about your daughter, Professor Richards…"

Alexandra jumped before the woman. "I'm her daughter. What's this about?" Yee ducked under her arm and chased Kate and me into the inner office. She again thrust the phone into Kate's face. I placed my hand on it and pushed it down.

"You're being rude, Ms. Yee," I raised my voice, hoping she would back off.

She ignored me: "Dr. Richards, would you comment about your daughter?"

Before Kate could say another word, Alexandra ran in, pushed the journalist onto the couch, and hovered menacingly over her. "What the hell do you want?" she demanded, breathing into her face.

Yee sat up and smiled triumphantly, again ignoring Alexandra and speaking to Kate: "It's not out there yet, and if you work with me, we can probably keep it that way for a bit. Very few people know…" The woman spoke confidently as she turned her gaze toward Alexandra, then to me, and then back to Kate, on whom her eyes rested. It was only then that I notice her piercing brown Eurasian eyes. I had not seen her before, but with those eyes and cheekbones and fancy haircut, she undoubtedly was on the Stream.

Yee smiled and lowered her voice, striking a less confrontational tone, now that she had us where she wanted: "If you and the Senator give me a family interview, I'll keep it quiet while you figure out how you want to frame the story before it breaks."

"What story?" I protested, hoping she might be bluffing. I turned toward Alexandra. "What's she talking about?"

"Cut the shit, Mr. Vannicelli!" Yee shook her head. "I'm not talking about her, and you know it. I'm talking about Rachel." She turned back toward Alexandra: "your half-sister. The one raised by your grandmother. *La Signora Grazia*," she added with a malicious smile and an exaggerated Italian accent.

Yee looked at Kate. "Do we have a deal?" It wasn't really a question.

***

"Senator Hernandez." Yee turned toward him as the Stream drone panned the family seated with him on a couch – Kate, Alexandra, and Rachel, who had flown in from London the day before. "You really had no idea? All those years?"

Hernandez said nothing at first, allowing the camera to pan the family again: the good Senator and three virtuous women sitting upright in conservative long dresses. After much discussion, we had decided to place the Senator between Kate and Rachel, so that he could hold both of their hands as needed for visuals.

I stood by the camera mount as the drone returned to it and docked. Randy, standing next to me, balanced his laptop on his arm watching a real-time focus feed that would reveal how well, or how poorly, things were going.

"That's right, Kim. I didn't know. Kate often had work and conferences in London, and she and her mother were always very close. So I never gave much thought, you know, to the fact that she went so frequently, and sometimes stayed on for several days." His voice was calm, and he smiled warmly at Kim – with not a trace of loathing in his eyes.

"Did she do the right thing, Senator?" Yee asked.

"Not only was it the right thing, it took courage and generosity…"

Yee cut Dick off and turned to Kate: "Why did you do it, Professor Richards? Surely there must have been a better option…"

Dick continued where he had left off: "She did it to protect my career. It was a big sacrifice made out of love. And she was a great mother to both girls…"

"Excuse me, Senator," Yee interrupted. "Your wife," she gestured toward Kate, "lied to you. Repeatedly. She concealed a child from her husband. For over two decades! Certainly, you must resent that. How can you still trust her?"

Dick took Kate's hand. "My wife has more integrity than anyone I know. Did she conceal Rachel from me? Yes. But she did it…" He smiled warmly at Rachel and deftly changed the subject: "You know, I am so thrilled to discover now that we have another daughter!" He patted Rachel on the hand and chuckled. She leaned toward him.

Hernandez turned toward the camera: "And let me say something else, lest anyone doubt who the selfish one was: If I had been less self-centered and ambitious – less narcissistic – let's call it what it was – as a young man, Kate would have had a better choice than the one I gave her. I'm not the victim here, Ms. Yee. If you feel like blaming someone, blame me."

"I'd like to add something," Rachel interjected. "My mum wasn't able to live with me when I was little, but I always knew she loved me. We spoke and played video games together all the time, and she visited me in London often. And my grandmother was – and is – wonderful. I had a very happy childhood. I always felt loved."

"What do you have to say for yourself, Professor Richards. In retrospect, would you have done it differently? Wouldn't it have been better to find a way to keep the girls together?" Yee looked at Kate with eyes that at least pretended to be kind.

"Of course I have regrets," Kate responded. "I regretted every day that I couldn't kiss Rachel's forehead when she came home from school. I hated having to lie to my husband, and to Alexandra. And of course, it would have been better if the girls could have grown up together."

"But," Alexandra reached over Rachel to take Kate's hand, "you chose the best option you had, Mom."

"We love you," Rachel shed what looked like a real tear, as she placed her hand on top of her sister's and kissed her mother on the forehead.

Hernandez nodded in agreement as he raised Kate's other hand to his lips. I noticed that he seemed content not to be the center of attention.

"Well," Yee continued. "Thanks to each of you for coming on the show, and for your willingness to share with America some intimate family matters. I know this can't have been comfortable for you."

Randy was smiling at his screen. I looked at the numbers over his shoulder and shot a thumbs up at Kate.

Yee continued: "I see we have a commercial break now, but when we return, I want to ask the Senator some questions about this switchgrass problem we hear so much about. Thank you all."

As soon as the red light went off, Kate, Rachel and Alexandra got up and marched past Yee without looking at her. Kate whispered something in Rachel's ear. Hernandez shuffled toward the journalist on the couch, keeping his eye on the camera to make sure it wasn't on.

"You're a real horse's ass, Yee," he sneered. She simpered back at him.

Randy ran onto the set and shoved his laptop at the Senator. We were in good shape.

***

Antonio slept on the front couch of the rented van, while Randy snored in the rear. I sat on a swivel seat, looking out the window at Iowa cornfields and listening to the conversation behind me:

"So there really are genetically modified pigs out there?" Hernandez asked Rachel.

"That's right, Senator Hernandez – I mean Dick. Um, what exactly am I supposed to call you?"

He smiled. "How about 'Dad?' I'm the closest thing you have to one, right?"

"Well, OK. Let's see how it works. Dad." She smiled back.

"You don't know what you're getting into," Alexandra deadpanned.

I turned toward them. Rachel had her mother's lips, green eyes, and thick, brown hair. Unfortunately, she had her unknown father's nose.

"So, Senator Dad, you signed up for CDC's biohazard alerts, saw something about the pig liberation raid, and decided to run with it on a national broadcast? Just like that? Bloody ballsy."

"Well, I was careful how I phrased it. But tell me, what's the deal with these pigs?"

Rachel leaned toward him. "Well, a startup called 'Gen-ethics' inserted a gene into pigs to ramp up their metabolism..."

"'Ramp up?'"

"...it sent their damn metabolism into overdrive! The idea these geniuses had was that the blood of nervous, muscular pigs would contain a cocktail of hormones that could be harvested to produce an anti-obesity drug for humans."

"'Gen-ethics,' you say?"

"Yeah. Kind of ironic, isn't it? Anyway, it didn't work, and the company went belly up two years ago."

"Pork-belly-up, you might say?" Dick smirked.

"So it seems that when the company folded, they left dozens of these crazy muscle-bound pigs unattended in a facility in Nebraska. When some animal-rights types calling themselves 'Animals 'R Us' found out about them, they had the brilliant idea to liberate them."

Kate coughed, without looking up from her Reader.

"Liberate them? As in..."

"Yeah, as in opening up the doors and letting them out. I mean, there have been wild pigs out there for decades, so what was the big deal, right?"

"Except that these weren't ordinary pigs..."

"More like huge, jumpy, voracious super-pigs. And now they're running around Nebraska and neighboring states, digging up farmers' fields and eating everything in sight. Seems they're rather amorous too."

"How many are there?"

"We believe there might be several thousand."

"THOUSANDS?!" Alexandra and I said simultaneously. Kate, in the back, had put down her reader and was looking out the window. She hadn't said anything, but I could tell she was listening to the conversation.

"And more every day! I told you they were randy buggers," Rachel continued, turning toward Kate. "Fornicate at the slightest provocation."

There was silence for a moment in the van as we all considered what this might mean.

Kate turned and stared at Rachel: "We should keep it quiet. Don't say a word. It'll come out on its own."

"That's right," I continued her thought. "With winter approaching, the switchgrass will die off, and Cranmore will think she's in the clear. Maybe we can even provoke her into saying we exaggerated the gen-mod threat?"

"And then…" Alexandra added, "Just before the primaries…"

"The snorting faces of nasty killer pigs will be on every monitor. Once the story gets out, reporters won't be able to resist showing ugly grunting monsters running amok, digging up farmers' fields and terrifying communities!" Dick smiled.

"Alarming, isn't it?"

Chapter Seventeen

Randy handed me his latest poll, and then slunk away through the hotel lobby, as if it were his fault. With the autumn frost, voters had forgotten about the switchgrass, and Cranmore had avoided making any more gaffes.

I crumpled the paper and shoved it into my pocket. It wasn't Randy's doing that we were losing. If anyone was to blame, it was the Senator's Chief Strategist – the one who had agreed to sit on the pigs story until Cranmore put her foot in her mouth again, which she never did.

That strategist, unfortunately, was me.

So when the Neanderthal man approached my table in the hotel lobby, slouching and slovenly, stinking of cigarettes and wearing a red "Real American" cap, I was in no mood to deal with assholes or suffer fools.

"I don't wanna be an asshole," the fool said.

I squinted, tilted my chair back against the wall, and lifted a foot onto the table, showing him the sole of my shoe. He had grease on his shirt and dirt under his fingernails.

"Like I said," the caveman grunted, tapping on the green "Hernandez for President" poster beside me. "I don't wanna be an asshole, but your guy's a fucking tree-hugger." I stared at him.

"Senator Tree-hugger! Mr. Clean!" He chuckled at his own unstoppable wit.

"I don't suppose you have studied rhetoric, have you?" I asked, without altering my facial expression. He looked back at me with stupidity in his close-set eyes.

"What I mean is, your sentence structure suggests a limited familiarity with semiotics or linguistic construction." I allowed a hint of contempt to spice my gaze.

"Huh?"

"For example, while I won't comment on your ethos or pathos, I do have an issue with your logos. Among rhetoricians, it is generally agreed that when one begins a sentence with a subordinate clause – in this case your assertion that you would prefer not to be an asshole – one should seek to maintain that commitment at least until the end of the sentence."

"What?"

A smile crossed my face. A scowl grew on his.

"You been outside? Global warming don't exist, you know!" He gestured triumphantly toward the window, where falling snow apparently proved his point.

"Of course you don't believe in global warming. That would require knowing what a globe is."

He grabbed the table's edge and leaned toward me. "You making fun of me?"

I turned my head to evade his cigarette breath, and returned my foot to the floor, eyeing the door to my left.

"Maybe you think I should shut up, Mr. Smart-Ass?"

"Of course not," I sneered, the momentary joy of sarcasm prevailing over my general aversion to being savagely beaten by a pre-human. "Please keep talking. Sooner or later you'll say something intelligible."

I scouted my escape path, reasoning that I could outrun him, even if he didn't trip over his knuckles.

"Mr. Clean, he wants to take our jobs away with all his environment crap. You hear me?"

"I hear you. It's just that I couldn't care less what you think."

The Missing Link lunged at me, but I pushed the table forward, knocking him to the floor, and burying him under "Hernandez for President" lapel pins and lawn signs. I ran up the stairs to Dick's green room. The Secret Service agent posted by the door stepped aside to let me enter.

"You're winded." Kate stated matter-of-factly, looking me up and down, before turning back to the talking heads on the wall monitor chatting about the presidential debate due to start in an hour. "Something exciting going on downstairs?"

"Not really. Just discussing climate policy with one of Canterbury's science advisors."

"Huh?"

I turned to Hernandez and placed a hand on his shoulder: "How's it going? You ready?" The smile on his face told me he was in a good mood – Randy must have been afraid to show him the poll.

"Don't waste any time out there, Senator. You're behind."

"We're going to pull ahead soon," he stated. "The undecideds will break our way. You'll see. Tonight, we play our ace in the hole."

I noticed his use of "we" and "our," as if it wasn't all about him. Kate, seeming to read my mind, smiled.

"Ace in the hole?" I asked. He stared blankly at me, but the corners of his mouth suggested he was suppressing a grin. "I'm glad you're relaxed, Senator, but I must point out that your poll numbers have been slipping. Once the switchgrass died off…"

Kate sniffed. "Don't worry, Marco. Everything's under control."

"Under control?" I turned toward her. "We're losing everywhere! And the debate moderator, that shithead Lester Downs, hates us!"

At that moment, Rachel and Alexandra walked in, arm-in-arm, chuckling.

"All set." Rachel winked at Kate.

"He's gonna do it!" Alexandra hugged her father from behind and looked at me.

"Who'll do what?" I asked.

"Lester Downs! Sorry we didn't have time to consult you, Marco, but Rachel had a brilliant idea, and we needed to get to him right away, before the debate."

"What are you talking about?"

"Let's just say we made Lester an offer he couldn't refuse." Alexandra lifted her chin and looked out the window.

"You threatened him?"

"Of course not!" She turned back toward me. "We merely handed the narcissistic creep a very interesting report – and pointed out that if he breaks the story during the debate, he could go down in history as the one who asked the famous question that everyone remembers. You know, like Howard Baker: 'What did the President know and when did he know it?'"

They all chortled. I wasn't angry about having been left out of something important – if whatever they were laughing about could turn it around, it was fine with me.

"So what's this report that's going make such a difference?" I asked.

Hernandez' tone was affectionate as he put his arm around me and said: "You really are a thick motherfucker aren't you, Vannicelli?"

So now I was the caveman – a role I wasn't used to. I felt something approaching empathy for the idiot I had just fled from in the lobby. Must suck not to have a clue what's going on around you all the time.

"I'll give you a hint, dummy," he stared into my eyes as he put his face up to mine. "Oink, oink. Snort, snort."

***

President Cranmore and Hernandez took the stage from opposite sides, meeting in the middle, in front of the host's table. Kate sat on a small chair, just offstage. I stood behind her. Alexandra, Rachel, and Randy were already in the spin room, getting ready to suck up to journalists.

The candidates smiled at each other and then waved to the audience. I had coached Dick to stoop slightly when extending his hand toward the diminutive president, and to give her a big, friendly smile. This would both call attention to their size difference and make him look gracious.

He choreographed it perfectly. Hernandez one, Cranmore zero.

She smiled and nodded as they shook hands, but Dick quickly scored another point by holding on several seconds, to confirm his physical domination – skillfully hiding this power play behind his famous smile. Two to zero, Hernandez!

He then surprised me by cupping his left hand over their handshake. I would never have advised him to make such a high-risk move, as it could be seen as an attempt to intimidate his smaller opponent, and might backfire, especially among women voters. But he pulled it off with grace, behind gentle eyes and that amazing set of teeth, projecting warmth rather than domination – and leaving Cranmore with a Hobson's choice: she either could add her left hand to the mix (thereby ceding to his leadership) or leave it dangling helplessly by her side (making her look unfriendly). She chose the former option, covering her defeat with a big smile, as if she were enjoying herself.

Kate missed nothing. She spun around and gave me a thumbs up, before turning back to the show. I felt hot, so I took a handkerchief from my pocket and wiped my brow.

The candidates walked to their podiums and nodded to the millions of voters behind the TV camera, as if to say "Yes, of course you want to vote for me!" Hernandez looked confident and relaxed. Cranmore smiled a bit too much.

I looked at my soaked handkerchief, wondering how it could have gotten so hot so fast in the studio.

"President Cranmore and Senator Hernandez." Lester Downs beamed for the camera, as if he were the main attraction. "Thank you for being here tonight, so that primary voters next week can assess your very different visions for the Democratic party."

"Very different visions…very different visions…." His voice wobbled and echoed. "Verrrry difffffferent viiiissssions." Was there a problem with the sound system? Downs was only a few feet from me, but he sounded far away. His lips moved slowly – gibberish came out. No surprise there, I thought, but why couldn't I move my arms? Was I in a straitjacket?

The Environmental Alarmist   111

I bumped the back of Kate's chair. She turned toward me as my legs buckled and I began to fall. I heard the candidates, in the distance, giving opening statements as Kate's arms lowered me gently into what had been her seat.

How strange, I thought, as I blacked out. This is the campaign's make-or-break moment – and I don't care.

***

I felt at peace, pleasantly cool and comfortable. Kate's hands on my neck felt good – like a warm blanket on a chilly night. The little girl in the floral dress pulled on my pant leg. *"Marco,"* she cried. *"La dobbiamo trovare!* We have to find her!"

She needed my help to find her mother. The child turned and ran through the outdoor market, past the fruit vendors calling out the virtues of their goods in Cremona dialect. I ran after her. I wanted to help the little girl. She was what I cared about – not the campaign or the election. I wanted her to find her mother.

I had had this vision so many times over the years that I knew what came next: I would call to her as she ran by the fishmongers, but she wouldn't hear me. She would keep running. Running away. In the wrong direction.

But this time, I didn't call out – I somehow knew that wasn't what she needed. I watched her shrink to a dot behind a market stall festooned with cheeses and *prosciutti.*

I walked calmly to the stand, knowing that everything would be fine. An elderly lady smiled and handed me a piece of pecorino. She patted me on the head and called me a *bravo ragazzo,* a good boy. I smiled up at her.

***

I opened my eyes, lifted my head, and smiled at Kate kneeling in front of me, her back to the stage. I felt calm, very calm. Preternaturally serene. The debate we had worked so hard to prepare Hernandez for was taking place right behind her, but we ignored it as I took her hand:

"I know where her mother went!" I said. "The little girl, Kate! She's OK. She's in no danger! No danger at all!"

Kate smiled. She couldn't possibly have known what I was talking about, but somehow, she understood. It made no sense, but it made perfect sense.

"And... I remember her name!" I gasped. In the distance, the audience was clapping at something Hernandez had said.

"Maria! The girl's name is *Maria*!"

"Yes, Marco. Of course."

I closed my eyes again and listened to the words of an old song running, for some reason, though my head:

"No, no, no, non crederle, non gettare nel vento in un solo momento, quel che esiste fra noi. No, don't believe her, don't throw into the wind, in one moment, what exists between us."

***

"Pigs? Mr. Downs? Did you say 'pigs?'" President Cranmore asked, the stage-lights reflecting off her forehead and highlighting her curly black hair.

I was seated and managed to focus again on the debate. Kate had pulled up another chair and sat beside me.

"That's right, Madam President," Downs repeated. "Aggressive pigs rampaging across the Midwest, tearing up fields and terrorizing people."

"I'm sorry, but haven't there always been wild pigs?"

My eyes followed Kate's across the stage to Dick's face – a convincing expression of grave concern concealed his joy.

"Well, Mr. Downs," Cranmore was trying to sound both involved and informed. "My administration monitors these matters carefully. You know, wild pigs are nothing new..."

Kate and I turned to each other, astounded that she had said it a second time.

Downs pounced: "These pigs ARE something new, President Cranmore. They're almost the size of bison, aggressive and destructive. They appear to be genetically modified mutants – like that switchgrass that Senator Hernandez keeps talking about...."

"Well, all I can say is that we will – we are – looking into this, Mr. Downs. I assure you, my administration takes these matters very seriously..."

"Excuse me, Madam President," Downs interrupted her with the zinger he hoped would put him in the history books: *Can you tell me exactly which office in your administration is responsible for monitoring giant, genetically modified pigs?"*

Cranmore stared at the journalist for several seconds. She had no answer to his question, and the world knew it. The President was melting down in front of millions of viewers, with just a week to go before the first primaries.

Downs continued, "You thought Senator Hernandez was being hysterical about the switchgrass. You called him an alarmist. An environmental alarmist. Do you think this pig thing is just another example of him spreading ridiculous rumors? Madam President?"

A ten-second eternity of deafening silence followed, before Cranmore made the biggest mistake of her life:

"You know my views on this. I stand by my statement, Mr. Downs."

"What statement are you referring to?"

"What I said about my opponent, Senator Hernandez! He thinks every problem is a crisis! We need to keep calm! Be sensible! Prioritize! We need to assess matters carefully before shouting 'fire!' and scaring people!"

Downs took a sheet of paper off his table and read it, trying not to smirk. It was a report from a local news outlet in Nebraska. As he read its account of rampaging pigs and damage to crops, Cranmore blanched.

The moderator then turned to Dick: "Senator, what do YOU make of this biohazard? Did you know about it?"

Hernandez looked into the camera and made eye contact with the nation. His countenance was solemn; his posture erect. He took his time. Then he spoke:

"Lester, I wouldn't call it a 'biohazard.' I rather would call it the inevitable result of poor regulation and lax oversight. I brought the switchgrass problem to the nation's attention some months ago, not because I hate science or want to stop genetic research, but because I want this important research to be done safely. The President dismissed me as 'an environmental alarmist' at the time."

He paused briefly so that the cameras could focus on his rival's wincing face.

"I couldn't understand why she thought that, but she did. For me, it wasn't about curtailing legitimate, important research. It was about protecting people, protecting our children. Protecting our farmers – many of them going bankrupt because of an invasive weed that we needed – and still need – to deal with. But unfortunately, the President didn't take that problem seriously. She said she wanted more evidence. And now, some of our trading partners are threatening to ban US agricultural exports until we get the problem under control. Think about what that will mean for our economy! For our farmers!"

He paused and turned slowly toward the President. "Sally...is it enough now?" He regarded her with kind eyes, the famous Hernandez smile, and a tender tone that made it sound almost like a gesture of friendship. "Do you have enough evidence now?" The question hung in the air for several seconds; Cranmore tried not to look panicked.

"Sally," he continued, "three years ago I agreed to serve as your EPA Director, because I thought you understood the need to address environmental problems *before* they became crises. But as the climate emergency has continued to damage..."

Lester Downs interrupted: "Senator, please answer the question. Did you know about the pigs? Yes or no, Senator?" Dick hesitated. Kate stood up.

"Yes, Lester. Because I monitor all environmental matters closely. And I asked my staff to look into it. I then called the EPA to ask what the administration was doing about it." He paused. "My calls were not returned."

I had no idea if this was true, but the look on Cranmore's face suggested it was.

Lester Downs turned toward her. "President Cranmore. Did you drop the ball on this?"

Sally Cranmore stared at Downs. She said nothing, but her eyes seemed to say: *"Et tu, Brute?"*

Chapter Eighteen

"In a word, Jesus! The Lord *Je-e-sus* called me to run for President!"

The bald white man with chubby red cheeks, sly dark eyes and beguiling smile leaned toward Lester Downs, who nodded knowingly as Jack Canterbury's press secretary shook her head on the split screen. The Chyron flashed across the bottom of the monitor: "Unreliable Source – Unverifiable claim – **Vestimate <10%**."

"Je-e-sus! I wish that idiot Zaricki would shut the hell up! Monitor off!" Hernandez barked. The screen went dark.

I sat on the edge of a chair facing him and placed a hand on his shoulder. With two days to go before the first primaries, the polls showed a dead heat between him and Cranmore. Of course he was on edge.

"Zaricki's an idiot," I said, "but he's Canterbury's problem, not ours."

"That's not the point!" The Senator's face was lined with concern. "Why can't this country ever learn from its mistakes?"

Alexandra and Rachel looked up from the table across the hotel room, but it was Kate who spoke: "Is it possible that someone is losing his taste for politics?" She paused, before lifting her gaze. "Or is it that my dear, lovely husband is seeing things from a new perspective?"

"What's that supposed to mean?" he asked. His voice was soft – I scrutinized his face, trying to judge what he might be thinking. Kate came over, sat next to me and leaned forward to take her husband's hands, regarding him intensely. His eyes, tearing up, shifted back and forth between us. Then he spoke:

"Zaricki represents everything that's wrong with this country. The ignorance. The thoughtlessness. The science-denialism. All this bible-thumping pisses me off even worse than Canterbury's brainless slogans. The planet is burning, cities are flooding, the oceans are dying – and to ice the goddamn cake, we've got giant, feral pigs and invasive switchgrass! And all that shithead can talk about is Jesus? As if it were up to Him, not us, to stop the planet from going up in smoke?!" He spoke with that earnest tone he usually brandished only when speaking in public.

Kate smiled. "Careful, love, your real you is showing!" She leaned forward to kiss his forehead, and a shy smile crossed his face. Alexandra and Rachel pulled up chairs on either side of him.

"You think maybe I'm coming down with something?" His smile broadened into a big toothy grin.

"You're not coming down with anything," Kate chuckled. She took his head in both of her hands. "You're rising above. And I'm very proud of you!"

"I still want to win..." he said.

The door swung open and Antonio and Randy ran in. They looked up at the wall monitor, surprised that it wasn't on, and then stared at the five of us huddled together.

"You didn't hear it?" Antonio asked me, breathing heavily.

"Hear what?"

"Zaricki! He just attacked the Senator on the Downs show. He said..." Antonio stopped and grinned.

"What?" I asked. Rachel pulled out her phone to check her news feed. Alexandra called the monitor on, where a well-dressed young man was explaining the virtues of 'Eco-jeans – 100% recycled.'

Antonio snorted as he spat it out: "He said Cranmore was right to call you an environmental alarmist!"

Kate jumped up. "Oh! My! God! Two days to go, and the rightwing loon just hugged Cranmore?"

"He told Lester Downs that Jesus came to him in a dream and told him to stop YOU from being elected! He said you're..." Antonio halted again, unable to contain his amusement.

"What?!" we all shouted.

Randy picked it up: "Zaricki just said, on the Stream, with millions watching, that you're doing the devil's work…" Randy started to crack up too, but then pulled himself together. "Seems you're a Satanist, sir. The leader of 'Mephistopheles' Environmentalist Legions on Earth,' or something. It made no sense…"

"It doesn't have to!" Kate and I said in unison, jumping up and high-fiving.

"Because when this goes viral…" She was shouting with glee.

"… Democratic voters…" Alexandra continued.

"…will rally to us!" Randy nodded.

Rachel looked up from her phone, laughing. "It's even better. Seems Canterbury's press secretary heartily agreed with him about your satanic malevolence! The whole Republican Party, it seems, thinks that…"

"…I'm afraid so, Senator," I continued her thought. "You're the official candidate of Beelzebub!"

"The Preferred of Perdition!" Alexandra guffawed.

"Remind me to send Zaricki a Halloween card, would you Vannicelli?" Hernandez deadpanned.

Kate pulled a bottle of bubbly from the mini bar. As she worked the cork, Rachel took out seven bio-cups and placed them on the table.

"You know, luv," Kate said as the bottle popped and she began to pour, "you always were a sexy devil…"

Alex kissed her father on the forehead and then wrinkled her nose:

"Gotta do something about that sulfur smell though."

Rachel piled on: "Agreed. Won't do when you meet the Royals."

As we passed the cups around, I raised mine to propose a toast: "To Senator Hernandez, the Environmental Alarmist – truly, if I might say so, the candidate from Hell!"

***

I almost didn't open the email. When it's the morning of the election and you're the Chief Senior Advisor on Everything to the guy surging in the polls, you get dozens every hour.

But I recognized the address – and the Subject Line said: "Good luck today, Marcolino!" – the nickname my mother had called me.

I opened it: "Bet you a bottle of *Barbera d'Asti* you pull it off! Love, Mary."

I typed a quick reply: "Thanks. It's been a roller coaster ride – and I'm pooped! Win or lose, once this is over, I'm going to need more than a glass of wine. More like a long Italian vacation!"

I hit send. Seconds later, I got a reply: "Well, over that bottle, maybe I could explain why you have exactly the right idea? You're going to find yourself more at home in Italy than you might ever imagine, my friend!"

I wondered what she meant.

***

"So, Senator Hernandez. Mr. Zaricki says you're a Satanist. Care to comment?"

Randy and I had warned the Senator that he had little to gain from doing the Lester Downs show the day before the primary election – the undecideds were breaking for us, so the sensible thing would be to lay low.

But he wanted one last chance to speak to the voters. When he explained why, Rachel and Alexandra surrounded him and then invited me into their group hug. What he wanted to do was courageous. It was risky. But it was the right thing.

"Look, Lester," he said, "I know you want me to talk about that silliness, or whatever the distraction *du jour* is. But I have more important things to say. This election isn't about Mr. Zaricki, or even about President Cranmore and me. It's about…"

"For the record, Senator, you do NOT deny being a Satanist?"

We had expected that line, and had come up with the perfect retort, but when I gestured from my position next to the camera, he ignored me. He was going to do it his way.

"I see no reason to deny ridiculous accusations. But let me tell you who I think Satan is. Mr. Downs."

"Call me Lester," he said with a malicious smile.

Hernandez was unphased: "Satan is continuing to burn fossil fuels while the seas rise and the planet burns. Satan is over-fishing and dumping plastics into the oceans. Satan is unleashing dangerous, invasive organisms into our environment. I've been fighting these evils all my life, *Mr. Downs*. Perhaps you should ask your corporate sponsors who the Satanists are."

"I would think a simple 'No, I'm not a Satanist' would do, *Senator*." Clearly, he was enjoying himself, and thought he had Hernandez where he wanted him. "Care to try again?"

The Senator kept it together: "Satan also is turning our backs on the men, women and children living in refugee camps because they've lost their homes to rising seas, and unbearable heat. Satan is putting up fences and walls to keep out these victims of our own recklessness. When instead we should be extending a helping hand…"

"So you think we should let them all in? Don't we need to defend ourselves from those who might do us harm?"

The Senator's eyes brightened. Downs, not realizing yet that he had taken the bait, pressed on: "You want us to throw open our borders too?"

Hernandez glared at him as he responded, speaking slowly: "My grandparents, who helped raise me and whom I loved with all my heart, came to this country escaping hardship, as have millions of other Americans. Then, as now, there were those who wanted to turn them away. To keep them out. To put up walls. People so fearful…"

He paused. I noticed his expression change from anger to sadness: "…people so fearful that they couldn't find their own humanity in the suffering of others."

As he took a deep breath, his expression changed once more, this time to solid resolve. He set the hook: "Would you have turned my grandparents away, Mr. Downs?"

"Look, I'm sure your grandparents were good people, but America just can't…"

"Can't what?"

Downs said nothing.

"Can you tell me how my grandparents were a threat to anyone? My loving, gentle, hardworking, honest grandparents, Mr. Downs?"

Downs' mouth maintained a confident smile, but there was fear in his eyes.

"I ask you again. America just can't what? America can't assist those in need? America is too small, in both senses of the word, to welcome new people?"

"We don't have endless resources, Senator."

The candidate smiled. "That's right."

Downs shifted again in his seat. He looked confused. Hernandez. continued:

"Precisely because we don't have endless resources, we need to change. We need to work together, to harness the energy and initiative of everyone. The environmental crises upon us will take sacrifice and commitment from all of us. We need everyone – those who have been here for generations and those who have just arrived – to build a sustainable economy. To protect and preserve our finite resources, not to despoil and pollute them. To rise above selfishness and shortsightedness and to work together to save our country, and our only planet."

Dick looked like he wanted to go on, but stopped to let the words sink in.

"There you go again, Senator. It always comes back to your simplistic, greeny dreams, doesn't it?"

"I'm not the one who's dreaming. I'm not the one sleepwalking toward catastrophe. The dreamers are those who, after all that has happened, continue to contradict the science. The dreamers are those who deny reality and refuse to change…"

Downs eyes darted left and right, then up and down until he thought he had found a new line of attack: "So, Senator, you think that it's President Cranmore's unwillingness to adopt your radical policies that is the devil's work?"

Dick chuckled. "The President and I are friends. She's a good person, and I know, having served in her cabinet, that she means well. Sally helped our country find its soul again after the turmoil that had torn us apart – and for that, we owe her a debt of gratitude."

He paused before pivoting to the message he had come to deliver:

"But time is short. We face multiple crises, of which the genetically modified pigs are only a particularly dramatic recent example. Past civilizations – the Easter Islanders, the Anasazi, the Maya and others – destroyed themselves because they denied environmental limits. Rather than accepting reality, they kept doing what they had always done – and they disappeared from the face of the Earth. They died, because they wouldn't change. And now, humanity risks doing the same – only this time it's global. This time, the entire planet is on the brink. Either we change, or humanity will go the way of the Maya and the Anasazi." He paused briefly. Downs said nothing. He continued:

"We will change, or we will destroy ourselves. And let me say it clearly, before the vote tomorrow – change will not be easy. It will be hard. It will require sacrifice – but the alternative is unthinkable. Thank you for your time, Mr. Downs."

Hernandez stood and extended his hand. Downs took it silently, and watched as the Senator walked off the stage, having broken the first rule of politics: never tell voters they need to sacrifice. I wondered if he had blown it. But then Randy shoved his tablet in front of my face. I smiled.

My phone rang and when I saw who it was, I answered.

"Brilliant, Marco! I'm so impressed by Hernandez. And proud of you, too!" she said. "Your ma is looking down and smiling!"

My head started spinning. Randy grabbed a chair and shoved it under me, next to the camera. I placed my head in my hands and watched little Maria in the floral dress run through the outdoor market. A little boy jumped out from behind a fruit-stand and tickled her. They ran away together, laughing.

I felt Randy shaking me gently. I looked up and he handed me my phone, which I must have dropped on the floor. Mary's name was still on the screen.

"Mary? You still there?"

"Everything OK?" she said.

"Just fine, thanks." My hands were shaking. "But I have to go. The Senator needs me. I'll call you later."

It was a lie, of course, but I didn't want to worry her. I hung my head between my legs, trying not to pass out again. Maria ran up the steps of a stone house that I somehow recognized. Her brother was with her. Her grandparents came to the door.

***

We huddled around the hotel room monitor as the primary election results trickled in. We couldn't believe what we were seeing. Dick was winning in every primary state.

Everyone was smiling, but there was no high-fiving or shouting. We watched quietly, with pride and satisfaction, but above all with a sense of awe.

Dick's phone rang. He looked at it and showed the screen to Kate before answering.

"Hello Madam President," he said. "Thank you for calling."

Chapter Nineteen

"Madam President, I can't tell you how much I appreciate what you're saying."

Hernandez leaned against the hotel room window, one hand pressing against the pane, the other holding his phone to his ear. His eyes followed a patch of cumulous clouds drifting eastward, and then reversed to watch some birds flying west. Cranmore said something I couldn't hear. Nodding, he turned toward us, leaving a moist handprint on the glass that faded as it dried. He was smiling, but it wasn't the smile of a victor. It was more like that of a sage.

"Of course, Madam President. We would be honored. Kate remembers your conversations fondly, and I am sure…"

Cranmore interrupted him. His eyes lit up and he started bouncing up and down on his toes and heels.

"That's…that's incredibly noble of you. I…" She interrupted him again.

"Certainly. Yes, of course. Rachel and Alexandra will be there too, Madam President."

He put the phone on speaker and pointed at it.

"And cut the 'Madam President,' crap, would you please?!" were the first words we heard. "Jesus Christ! Do you think I'm an idiot? Don't answer that question!" She chuckled. "Look, you just kicked my black ass, and I deserved it. I ran a shitty campaign, and you ran a brilliant one. Now let's pull this goddamn party together and teach those Republicans a lesson! I'm going to do everything I can to keep that troglodyte Canterbury out of this White House! Even if it means electing an insufferable smartass prick like you!"

Hernandez grinned and shot me a thumbs-up as he sat down next to Kate. She took his hand and squeezed it.

"And make sure you bring that Vannicelli, too! I want to meet the magician who helped you end my Presidency. I want to shake his goddamn hand! You always had an eye for talent, Dick, but the way you guys fooled me with this GMO shit was brilliant!"

"Without false modesty, Sally, we also got lucky. I mean, Zaricki…"

"That crazy idiot. Sure. But you made it close enough for his lunacy to matter." Cranmore paused. When she resumed talking, her tone had changed – she sounded almost wistful: "And there's something else I want to tell you. I've been in this business a long time. I could see the winds were shifting, that it was time for a change. When I was the Vice President…"

Suddenly she started shouting: "…and I gotta say that motherfucker Vannicelli has a great sense of optics!" She paused. "You know, speaking of which, how do you think it would look if I sent Marine One to pick you up? I mean, it's electric-solar and everything?"

"Let me think about it. I mean, Canterbury will say…"

"Bullshit! My people will let you know the details."

Hernandez was silent. Soon Cranmore resumed, in a soft, thoughtful tone: "You know what? I'm relieved. My work here is done. We did what we could to bring this country back to its senses. It was real hard, but we've turned the corner. This great nation is starting to look like the old, rowdy, lovable, dysfunctional, totally fucked-up but precious democracy we used to be…"

Unexpectedly, she started shouting again, causing Hernandez to push the phone away from himself: "Hey! I even had a nice round of golf last week with the Republican minority leader! Not a bad gal at all really, once you pull her head out of her ass!"

Once more, her tone softened: "So truly, my friend. It took this humiliation for me to realize it, but it was time for me to go. It's time for the Environmental Alarmist – or should I say the Environmental President? – to get going on the problems that festered while we fought over nonsense all those years. We did what we could to help heal this nation…"

"…and America owes you a huge debt of gratitude, Sally…"

"Shut the fuck up! I was talking! And I feel like I did a pretty good job, god-dammit! And now, I'm going to help my successor – that would be you, you piece of crap – unite the party, and teach that bastard Canterbury who the 'Real Americans' are!"

"I can't tell you how much this means to me."

"You're a horse's ass, Hernandez, but you ran one hell of a great campaign. See you tomorrow."

"Sally, I know this can't be easy for you, and I can't thank you enough for your grace and kindness. And, of course, your intriguing offer, which I'll discuss right now with Kate and Marco…"

"I said shut the fuck up!" The line went dead.

Hernandez grinned at us.

"What offer?" Kate and I asked simultaneously.

He turned toward the window, where clouds were parting, and a colorful sunset was forming. Placing both hands against the pane, he looked to the horizon. "You know what? I think I'll let the President tell you herself, tomorrow. At the White House."

"You told her you'd discuss it with us 'right away!'" Kate noted.

"Sure did." He faced us and smiled: "But I lied."

***

As Marine One descended toward the White House lawn, Alexandra took off her headset and gestured at me to remove mine so she could say something privately. It was my first time in an electric helicopter, and the gentle hum of the rotors was so soft that we could converse without headsets.

"I wanted to say just one thing…" She looked at me with moist eyes. "My dad is incredibly grateful for all you've done. He says the nicest things about you, when you aren't around. It's hard for him to praise people to their face, but he considers you to be his best friend." I wasn't surprised by her words, but I didn't know what to say.

She placed her hand on mine. "It's more than your work. He says you helped him see what matters…" She looked out the window. "You know what I mean? That this isn't a game? You taught me that too," she said as we touched the ground.

Out of the corner of my eye, I saw that Kate had removed her headset, and was gazing across the lawn toward the White House. Hernandez removed his and looked out the window at the gaggle of waiting reporters. As we disembarked and cleared the helipad, they started peppering him with questions. He waited for the one he wanted to answer:

"Senator," the young black-haired man in a hoverchair shouted, "do you plan to accept Jack Canterbury's debate offer?"

Hernandez flashed his killer smile and said he'd be happy to debate "the Republican nominee, after they pick one."

"You think Zaricki still has a chance?" the man asked. Canterbury had won every state primary, so it wasn't a serious question.

"That's for the Republicans to sort out, Mr. Degas-Adeyemi."

The journalist smiled, pleased no doubt that the presumptive Democratic nominee knew his name. Hernandez continued: "Of course, it would be nice if Mr. Canterbury were to clarify whether or not he agrees with Zaricki that I'm a devil-worshiper."

"So you're putting conditions on the debate, Senator? That would be unprecedented…"

"I agree," he said, before twisting the journalist's words to his advantage. "Calling your opponent a Satanist is indeed unprecedented. But once the Republicans have a nominee who wants to stop the name-calling, and start addressing the real problems this country faces, like the climate emergency and collapsing ecosystems…"

"And genetically modified pigs?"

"And GMO pigs, yes. Of course. In fact, the President and I will be discussing that today."

This wasn't exactly true, but by now Sally Cranmore had emerged onto the lawn and was waving to us, flanked by her two black Labrador retrievers, Mr. Spock and Bones. Hernandez waved back.

"Thanks, everyone!" he shouted as he strode past the journalists and toward his former rival, holding Kate's hand, the rest of us behind them. As we crossed the lawn, Cranmore opened her arms in a welcoming gesture. We stood back so that the cameras could capture the image of the current and future presidents embracing. Kate then introduced Rachel and Alexandra, amid abundant and perhaps even sincere smiles, as the Senator patted Mr. Spock on the head.

"And this, of course, is Mr. Vannicelli." Hernandez pushed me toward her. I extended my hand and she took it, smiling warmly with kind eyes. "A pleasure to meet you," she said, before leaning toward me and whispering in my ear.

I was surrounded by cameras, so I kept a straight face. I looked into her eyes – suddenly cold as ice and sparkling with conspiracy – and realized she wasn't joking.

***

"My fellow Americans…" Hernandez gazed out from the podium at the cheering delegates waving green "Hernandez!" signs and placards with the names of their states. His family stood behind him, beaming. Holding hands with Rachel and Alexandra was their grandmother, Grazia, who had flown in from Europe. I stood a few meters away, offstage. Kate turned toward me and wrinkled her nose.

"My fellow Democrats, I am humbled and honored to accept your nomination!" The crowd roared and the band played "Happy Days Are Here Again," as iconic images of FDR, JFK, Obama, Biden and Cranmore flashed behind the speaker. I thought back to that lousy speech Hernandez had given in Rome, and then the one I had written for him launching our campaign at the edge of the Grand Canyon. I allowed myself a bit of self-satisfaction, knowing that he was on his way to the White House, at least in part because I had done a good job.

But something had been bugging me these past three days of the convention, and as I surveyed the crowd, I wondered what it was. Was it those stupid state delegation signs? They were too small. Or too big. Too colorful. Annoyingly prosaic. Or was it the crowd itself? All those idiots bobbing up and down like Whack-a-moles? What were they smiling about? Who could care? They…bothered me. I saw little Maria running with her brother through a northern Italian piazza, but I was jolted back to attention as the Democratic nominee spoke:

"Friends. I know you're all eager to know who our next Vice President will be, but before I tell you, let me say a few words about a truly great American. Someone to whom we all owe an enormous debt of gratitude. Our great Democratic President, our great *American* President, and my dear friend, Sally Cranmore."

He gestured toward the backstage as she emerged and walked toward him, waving to enthusiastic applause. Even though the voters had rejected her, every delegate in the room knew she had been a terrific loser and was doing everything she could to unite the party.

"President Cranmore." He turned, but kept a respectful distance, so as not to call attention to the fact that he towered over her. "Our country has been through a lot over the past two decades. Many thought we would never heal after the Crisis – that the animosities and divisions were too deep and had gone on for too long. Your leadership, Madam President, your steady hand, your belief in the decency of the American people, President Cranmore…"

She leaned toward the microphone and interrupted him. "Call me 'Sally'" she said with a big smile. The crowd erupted in laughter and cheers. Hernandez hadn't expected this move, but he didn't miss a beat:

"Sally, you leave a proud legacy. This party and this nation will remember your presidency as a time of healing, and you have earned a place in history as someone who brought out the best in us and brought us back together. The leader who made decency and honesty and tolerance normal again. And who taught us the real meaning of patriotism. You taught us that patriotism isn't about being better than other people – it's about being better than we ourselves have been. It's not about lording it over others – it's about rising above our own failures. And, above all, you taught us that patriotism is about unselfishness. It's about caring – about putting other people before ourselves. You taught us a vital lesson – and we are a better nation today because of your leadership. Thank you for bringing out the best in us, President Cranmore! Because that's what great leaders do!"

I winked at Kate and she winked back, no doubt thinking the same thing that I was: this wasn't just rhetoric. He meant every word.

The convention applauded for several minutes as Cranmore and Hernandez smiled and waved. When the applause started to dim, he raised both hands to calm the crowd to silence.

"And now, my fellow Democrats, allow me to proudly present to you the next Vice President of the United States." He gestured to the backstage, as if someone were about to emerge. When no-one did, he nodded at Cranmore, who approached him. He put his arm around her shoulder, and she put her arm around his waist. Grinning broadly, they raised their other arms together and waved.

As the delegates realized what was happening, they went wild with cheers and applause. Dozens of green Hernandez/Cranmore signs rose around the arena. Confetti fell and the band played "Together We Can Change the World."

Chapter Twenty

Randy handed me his laptop and pointed at the results of his latest poll, which showed our lead over Jack Canterbury growing. "Amazing what a few thousand rampaging monster pigs can do for the right candidate," he grinned.

It also didn't hurt that the Republicans were running a truly awful campaign. Zaricki – now a Fox News host and suddenly Canterbury's biggest fan – was holding weekly "debates" among "theological experts" on whether one could be both "Christian Pure White" and "Environmentalist Dark Green." Yes, really. They went there. And when asked directly in an interview if his opponent was a devil-worshiper, the best Canterbury could come up with was that "not every environmentalist is a proven Satanist."

This idiocy gave us a perfect excuse not to debate, but Dick was determined. "I don't want to win just because of the pigs! Or because Canterbury is a blithering idiot," he said, putting his chamomile tea on the office table and turning toward Kate, Alexandra and me. "I want to win because people are ready for big change. And for that we need a mandate."

President Cranmore, on the wall monitor, shook her head: "Mandate, schmandate! You're cruising toward a landslide, Senator. That'll be all the mandate you need. If Canterbury wants to keep shooting himself in the foot, I say stay out of his way!"

The Senator responded in a respectful tone, explaining why he disagreed: "Politically, you're right, Sally. But this isn't politics as usual. This is a historic opportunity to make long-overdue changes. But people need to know that's what they're voting for."

Cranmore threw her hands up: "I may still be the Prez, my friend, but you're the boss. And maybe you're right. In any event, we're going to win no matter what you do."

"What does everyone think?" Kate asked.

They all looked at me, and I gazed back, but I didn't see them. I was a child again, running through an Italian piazza with Maria and her brother – Enzo. I remembered his name! We were laughing. Their grandmother, *our* grandmother, held my hand so I wouldn't fall. She lifted me up, kissed me on the cheek, and handed me to my mother. I was happy.

"Marco?" Kate asked, jolting me back to the office.

"You're who you are, Senator." I heard myself say. "Tell the voters the truth. Explain where you want to go, and why they should follow."

Alexandra and Kate rose and walked around the table. As they passed, Kate squeezed my shoulder and Alexandra patted me on the head. They stopped behind Hernandez, and Kate put her hands on his shoulders. "He's not just another pretty face, is he?" She looked toward me as she put her cheek to his.

"You saying I'm not pretty?" He turned his head toward Kate, looked at her cross-eyed, and stuck out his tongue.

"So, what exactly are you going to say, beautiful?" I asked, even though I knew the answer.

"You know what I'm going to say. I'm going to say we have to change. Not just some policies. And not just around the edges. We have to reassess everything. Change our attitude. Reassess our lifestyles. The denialism must end. The mindless, wasteful consumerism must end."

Kate eyes lit up: "'Make Gluttony Un-cool Again!' Hey! There's a slogan!"

"Got a better one." Alexandra grinned: "A very smart alarmist I know said it: 'Man does not weave this web of life. He is merely a strand of it. Whatever he does to the web, he does to himself.'"

"A bit long for a slogan, but the right idea." The father put his arm around his daughter and looked out the window at the setting sun. "It's taken too long, and much damage has been done – more than one administration can repair. But maybe people are ready to start down a new path. I'm going to spell out the sacrifices we all will need to make."

***

Alexandra and I walked across the backstage toward Kate and Rachel, already seated on the couch. Their gesticulations suggested they were having an intense exchange of views. I wondered what they might be arguing about, but when they saw us, they smiled and gestured toward the couch. The candidates were already on stage, at their respective podiums – Dick looking relaxed and confident, and Canterbury, bouncing nervously on his heels as if he'd just snorted Adderall laced with meth. Across the stage, some of his people were standing in a line, like soldiers waiting for inspection, staring at the moderator shuffling papers at her desk. We waved politely across at them, but they didn't wave back.

Our couch was large, soft, and inviting, and as we plopped ourselves down, we started chatting, as if preparing to watch a game in a pub, rather than a live presidential debate mere feet away. I held up a bottle of Spumante and my friends nodded their strong approval of the suggestion.

"Good evening," the moderator began, "and welcome to the Presidential debate between the Republican nominee, Jack Canterbury… (polite applause from the audience) and the Democratic nominee, Dick Hernandez (louder applause). I'm Yamiche Nguyen-O'Donnell, and I will be moderating…"

I worked the cork. Mary had sent me the bottle, with a sweet but cryptic card addressed to "the new Marcolino." When the cork popped, the moderator glanced toward me before continuing her introduction. I filled everyone's glass as the candidates made opening statements, to which we paid no attention at all. We knew ours by heart and knew what dribble we could expect from Canterbury. I raised my flute to propose a toast, but before I could, Alexandra spoke:

"Been a long, strange trip, hasn't it?"

I lowered my glass a bit and nodded. "It has indeed." Little Maria and Enzo flashed through my mind. They were smiling at me. "And I think it's changed us all, for the better."

"No shit!" Kate interjected. "And don't think it was easy!"

We turned toward her, chuckling – we knew what she was getting at. Kate was not one to brag, but she had been our guiding light. I lifted my glass, but before I could propose a toast, some commotion on the stage grabbed my attention.

"Mr. Canterbury!" the moderator shouted. "Please return to your podium!" With our glasses in the air, we beheld the bizarre spectacle of Canterbury waving a big, wooden crucifix in the Senator's face, as if he were Count Dracula. Hernandez stood behind his podium, trying to look concerned, but he must have been delighted. I lowered my glass. Kate put her arm on mine as we took in the spoof unfolding on stage. She giggled first, but soon we all were tittering with delight and sipping our Spumante. It was dry, crisp and refreshing.

"Do you worship the Prince of Darkness, Senator?!" Canterbury shouted, his voice cracking with righteous indignation. Hernandez looked at him impassively, no doubt wondering if the man had completely lost his mind.

"Do you renounce Satan and all of his deeds? Why won't you say you choose the Lord?"

To the camera, Canterbury may have seemed confident in his assault, but I was close enough to see the panic in his eyes – he looked as desperate as he must have been to pull such a prank. No doubt, his polling showed he might lose even the deep South.

"This is what happens when all you have left is your base," I said matter-of-factly, shaking my head and tilting my glass toward Kate's. She touched it with hers.

"Your base of screaming, bat-shit crazy lunatics!" Alexandra chuckled, downed her entire flute, and pushed it toward me for a refill.

"Mr. Canterbury!" Nguyen-O'Donnell stood and leaned over her desk. "I insist that you respect the rules and return to your podium!" Dick stood still, smiling beatifically.

"Mr. Canterbury!" the moderator shouted again. He ignored her and continued to wave the crucifix. She started around the desk toward him.

"Could I have some more too, luv?" Rachel asked, tilting her class toward me. I began pouring.

"Nice…" I said, pointing at her silver and coral earrings. "From New Mexico?"

"Good guess!" she smiled back at me. "Got them in Santa Fe! Navajo, I think."

The crowd gasped. I stopped pouring to turn again toward the stage, where Nguyen-O'Donnell had run up behind Canterbury and grabbed his shoulders with both hands.

"This is getting good, isn't it?" Alexandra guffawed, taking the bottle from me and filling her sister's glass and then her own.

"He's got this," Kate said calmly, standing next to me. "Watch what he says now."

"Thank you, Mr. Canterbury," Hernandez began, "for giving me the opportunity to clarify my beliefs…"

"I didn't ask you to clarify!" He was still holding up the crucifix, but his hand was shaking and Nguyen-O'Donnell was pulling him back. "I asked you to renounce Satan! To say you love the Lord! Is there some reason you cannot do so, Senator? Does the devil own your soul?!"

Hernandez extended his hand and placed it on the crucifix. "May I have that, please?" he said, in a calm voice. Canterbury hesitated a moment but then let go. Hernandez admired it as Nguyen-O'Donnell escorted Canterbury back to his podium. She mumbled something at him before returning to her seat.

"Indeed a beautiful crucifix," he said, holding it up and smiling kindly at his adversary. "Who made it?" Canterbury stood mute.

"Don't worry, I won't steal it!" the Senator said in a good-natured tone, as he placed the crucifix on his podium. There was some chuckling in the audience.

"You know why it's beautiful to me, Jack?" He put his hands on the podium and leaned forward toward his opponent, smiling with his eyes. "It's beautiful because it shows the love and talent of a fine artist. And it reminds me of my grand-parents, who were devout Catholics, and who derived much strength and comfort from their faith."

"The voters aren't interested in your grandparents, Senator!" Canterbury howled. "They want to know who YOU are!"

"Fair enough. Let me tell you who I am…"

"Just answer one, simple question! Do you worship Satan or not? Why can't the Senator answer that question?" he turned toward the camera, as if he had won the argument.

Hernandez also faced the camera. "Fine. Let me state it for the record that I do not worship Satan. I do not worship the devil. I never have and never will."

"Well, finally we get an answer!" Canterbury said. "Why did it take so long?"

"It took so long because such absurd accusations don't warrant anyone's atten-tion." Dick's voice was calm, steady and reassuring. "The American people want this campaign to focus on reality, on issues that matter. They want clean water, clean air, clean food, clean jobs. They want us to address the climate crisis and the green flies. They are concerned about invasive switchgrass and GMO pigs. They know that things are out of balance, that our gluttonous lifestyle is unsustainable. They know we need to change our attitude toward the natural world."

"There you go again, Senator, with your greeny propaganda. As if the good Lord would allow us to destroy His creation. You may not be a Satanist, sir, but Satan laughs every time you spout off all your environmentalist nonsense. All your 'sustainability' stuff is Satan's way of turning us away from God. Real Americans don't believe we need to change what made this country great. Freedom, you know…"

Hernandez waited while Canterbury rambled on, shouting slogans until he ran out of them. The Senator then stood silently so that his opponent's foolishness might hang in the air. Canterbury squirmed behind his podium.

Finally, Hernandez spoke: "So, what was it you said? Something about sustain-ability being 'Satan's way of…? Of what?'"

Canterbury sputtered: "All this 'sustainability' stuff is Satan's way of distracting us from God's one true path. You can't spell 'sustainability' without 'S-A-T-A-and N,' you know!" He chuckled weakly, before looking down and shuffling an imaginary paper around on his podium while running his other hand back and forth over his bald head. The room was silent.

Hernandez waited again before speaking.

"Mr. Canterbury," Dick ran his fingers through his thick, black hair. "Thank you for explaining your views. I'm sure you hold them sincerely. But could I ask...?

The moderator – whom everyone seemed to have forgotten about – interrupted: "Excuse me Senator Hernandez. I have allowed the two of you to run on for some time, but now may I remind you that this debate has rules, and that I am here to ask the questions?"

"Of course," he said, smiling politely. Canterbury looked relieved.

"So, it seems to me," Nguyen-O'Donnell began, "that Mr. Canterbury sees a conflict between environmentalism and his religion. Is that correct, sir?"

"The Lord gave us the soil to plow. He gave us the Earth to utilize. It was his gift to us. It says so in the Bible. He told us to 'go forth and multiply,' to make of his bounty what we would."

"Thank you. Now, Senator Hernandez, if I am not incorrect, you have a different view?"

He looked into the camera as he spoke: "Thank you. Well, I agree that God gave the Earth to us. But I also believe that God gave us to the Earth. We aren't above this world. We are part of it. As a very wise person said, years ago in 2019, 'Let us hear the cry of the earth, wounded in a thousand ways by human greed. Let us allow her to remain a welcoming home...'"

Canterbury jumped: "There you go again, with your Native American, New Age, touchy-feely-greeny..."

"Actually, that was Pope Francis," Hernandez said without a trace of "gotcha" in his voice.

He continued: "Leaders of all traditions have stressed that we must live in harmony with nature. One Buddhist philosopher put it this way: 'We are the environment. The non-human elements are our environment, but we are the environment of non-human elements, so we are one with the environment.'"

Canterbury inhaled as if he were going to interrupt again, but then exhaled. Hernandez looked at him kindly, and then back into the camera to deliver the message he had been working up to:

"The great Tolstoy wrote: 'One of the first conditions of happiness is that the link between man and nature shall not be broken.' This belief has motivated me all my life. Everyone who votes for me should know they will be voting for someone who believes we must construct a new relationship with the natural world. And that we will be happier for it. Our civilization has accomplished much in recent centuries. Our technology has produced great wealth and scientific breakthroughs. But we have been late to recognize that the power of our technology requires that we use it carefully. We need to change from a mentality of exploitation of nature, to a mentality of cherishing it, protecting it, and living within the limits of what the planet can sustain. Because we are part of this planet. We are part of nature. How many times has the Earth called out to us in pain, seeking to remind us of this fact? The climate and food crises, the Corona pandemic, the collapse of wild fisheries, the antibiotic emergency – we ignored warning after warning – and as a consequence we endured disaster after disaster – because we failed to change our ways. Because we clung to a way of thinking whose time had passed…"

He stopped and looked into the camera to make sure his point was lost on no one: "We need to change how we think, and how we live. So that we *can* live. To every voter I say this: if you believe that I am wrong, if you believe that we do not need to change, then do not vote for me. If you believe we should see this planet as a resource to exploit, rather than a home to cherish, then you should vote for my opponent, Mr. Canterbury. But if you are ready for change and understand that it will not be easy or painless, then please join me in making that change. Because I will dedicate my Presidency to working with you to build a new, better, happier relationship with the natural world."

A silence descended over the audience. Canterbury said nothing. As Nguyen-O'Donnell thanked Hernandez and a gentle but sustained applause began, Kate, Rachel and Alexandra placed their glasses on the table and smiled at Dick on the stage. He smiled back.

My phone rang. I looked at it and answered.

"Well hello!" I grinned. "Hey! Thanks for the Spumante! And what's this 'New Marcolino' thing?"

"Congratulations again, my friend. Check your email and call me when you can. I am so proud of you!" was all Mary said. The line went dead.

***

After the debate, and then the spin room, we went out to dinner. Everyone was cheerful, even giddy, at the restaurant, but whenever Antonio or Randy tried to discuss the election or the polls or the pigs, Kate steered the conversation back to how happy she was to share this moment with friends. No one mentioned what we all knew – the election was over. And perhaps an era was over. Dick was going to become President in January. The only question was how big our victory, and how clear our mandate, would be.

I was exhausted and sleepy when I got back to my hotel room hours later, but as I crawled into bed, I picked up my phone to read Mary's email. Her text was short: "See attached, Marcolino" followed by a smiley face. I opened the attachment. It was a photo of my mother and me when I was a toddler, holding hands in an Italian piazza. Behind us, were four other people – a boy and a girl, sitting on a stone bench with an elderly couple. I remembered the photo of her parents that Ma always kept on her mantle.

I pulled my knees to my chest, placed my head in my hands, and cried.

***

It was Christmas, and we were hard at work. The weeks since the election had been a whirlwind of activity as we worked on assembling a new administration. I stood at the window in the Executive Office Building and looked at the White

House, which would become my friends' new home in a few weeks. I wondered how long they would still need me.

There was a knock on the door.

"President-Elect Hernandez?" the Secret Service agent entered and handed her phone to him. "President Cranmore, sir." He tapped the agent's phone with his and waved the agent away. She smiled and exited.

"What's up, Sally?" Hernandez asked. His face dropped.

"Mount Rushmore? Are you fucking shitting me? Is this your idea of a joke?!" He put the phone on speaker for my benefit.

"Not a joke, Dick, I'm afraid. A bunch of them broke through the fences and started tearing the visitor center apart. Seems one of them actually got to the summit and took a dump over the edge. Landed on Lincoln's nose! Too bad Trump never got his face up there, huh?" she laughed. "The police seem to have the situation under control, but, needless to say, the optics of wild pigs shitting all over the Great Emancipator on Christmas Day are less than ideal. What do you want to do about this?"

For the first time ever, I saw Dick Hernandez speechless.

"Dick? You there?"

"Yeah. Um, would it be asking too much if I let you take this one? I mean, I'm sure you can handle it better than I could."

"No problem, my friend. I'll make a statement. I'm still President, and you've got a full plate. But if I could give you some advice, don't expect the Senate Republicans to be too helpful in dealing with this, or anything else. I called the leader, and she could hardly conceal her joy. Made every stupid excuse she could think up on the spot as to why she 'needed time' before they could approve any funding. These pigs got you into office, my friends. But on January 20th at noon, I'm sorry to say, you're going to own the whole pigsty. We'll keep working on it, my friend, but it seems some things never change."

Epilogue

The truth is never pure, and rarely simple.

— Oscar Wilde

Mary placed her wine on the table. "Your mother made this dress for me." she said, touching her shoulders. "After all these years, it still fits! Well, sort of," she smiled. "I let it out a bit."

I remembered Ma at her machine, sewing dresses and blouses for herself, and little boy suits for me. I recalled the pride on her face — was it for me or for her handiwork? — when she showed me my graduation gown and Harvard doctoral hood.

Mary twiddled the neck of her glass, glancing briefly at the well-dressed couple at the next table, before leaning in toward me: "I need to say something. Something important Ma told me, years ago. She swore me to silence..."

"I know what you're talking about," I heard myself say.

Mary's eyes widened; she shifted on her seat. "Um. So, um, what I wanted to say is that after you...after we...broke up..."

"Nice of you to put it that way, considering that I abruptly ended our engagement, without explanation."

The woman at the next table leaned toward the man. He looked away. I wondered if they were married, or if this was another illicit Washington rendezvous.

Mary touched my hand. "Remember how, in our last year together, you threw yourself into your work? You..."

"... became an antisocial, tedious workaholic, who never had time for anything but his research? The guy who used work like a drug, to shield himself from reality?"

"Yeah, that's the one." She squeezed my hand, clearly relieved at my unexpected self-awareness. *"At first, when you withdrew, I thought it was me…"*

"It wasn't, of course. But you must admit, I was creative – hiding from the truth among the charms and talismans of the dark arts of propaganda?!"

"Your brilliant, subconscious sense of irony was never lost on me." She smiled. *"Look, Ma wanted to tell you this herself – but she was afraid of how you might react. She blamed herself…"*

"It wasn't her fault. Instead of allowing myself to see what I couldn't accept, I ran away. I ran from her, from you, and from myself!"

I turned toward the window and gazed toward the sky. "I've been running since."

I saw little Maria, alone in the Italian piazza, her hands on her hips. She turned and sprinted past the fishmongers. Then she stopped, and Enzo appeared beside her. Together, they beckoned me to join them.

Mary sat back and placed both of her hands on the edge of the table.

"After we broke up, Ma stayed in touch. She called every few months. Then, the calls stopped."

We looked at each other across the table.

"Don't you see?" She leaned toward me. *"After she died, her secret became MY secret! I didn't know what to do. Should I tell you? Did I have the right to tell you? Did I have the right not to? Would you forgive her if I did?"*

"Alexandra forgave Kate," I said. *"And I know Ma did her best." I rotated my wine glass first in one direction, then in the other.*

Maria and Enzo each took one of my hands, and the three of us ran across the piazza toward a statue of a man handing a violin to a child.

The woman at the next table opened her briefcase and handed the man what I imagined were divorce papers.

"You did your best too." Mary placed a hand on my shoulder.

"Yeah. Although arguably my best totally sucked!" My arm slipped, but Mary caught the glass before it spilled onto the white tablecloth. She laughed – that same

laugh I remembered from years ago, when the three of us would sit for hours around Ma's table after dinner, telling stories and jokes, and simply enjoying being together.

I ran through the piazza with Maria and Enzo, giggling and dodging one another, until we came to the statue. An elderly couple stood beside it. Church bells rang – I gazed up at a tall clocktower.

"It's time for me to stop running, Mary." I looked into her eyes.

The man at the next table took out a pen and signed the papers.

"The truth was hiding in plain sight! That's why I ran. I couldn't accept it. That photo that Ma kept on the mantle..." I gazed out the window. "I'm not an only child, am I?"

"She told me you have a brother and sister, in Italy."

"Brother and sister" – the words echoed in my head with the church bells. I remembered the mantlepiece photo Ma kept of her parents. There were two children in the photo, sitting at my grandparents' feet. They had always been there in the photo, but I never could see them.

I stopped and took a deep breath. I smelled the sweetness of chocolate coming from the kitchen.

I ran to my grandparents, and we sat together on stone steps by the statue. My grandmother patted my head and asked if I wanted some chocolate.

"Did Ma ever explain why she left them in Italy and took me to America?" I asked. "Why she..."

"Go to Cremona." Mary smiled. "Go to Cremona."

The people at the next table stood to leave. They exchanged business cards and shook hands. I recognized the woman now, a lobbyist I had met once at a reception.

I rested my head on my palms and looked down at a tiny red stain on the tablecloth. That statue of the man with the violin – I remembered now, it was Antonio Stradivari, the great luthier of Cremona.

"Need anything?" the waiter asked. I waved him away, without looking up.

"Thanks, we're fine," Mary said politely.

"My father?" I asked. I felt her hand touch the crown of my head.

"All I know is that he died when you were a baby. Ma told me your sister was a doctor and your brother a luthier in Cremona. Here's the address of his shop." She pressed a piece of paper into my hand. "Nothing can hide from the AI."

I lowered my arms to the table and rested my head upon them. A powerful fatigue beckoned me to sleep. The waiter cleared the next table as I closed my eyes. Mary caressed my hair.

My brother, my sister, my grandparents and my mother sat with me by the statue of Stradivari. We gazed across the piazza at the belltower and ate bread and chocolate together. My grandfather let me dip a finger into his wine. It tasted terrible, but I loved him. I loved them all.

***

A few days later, I left for Italy. On the way to the airport, as the cab passed the White House, I got a text from Kate: "Can you talk?"

I called on the taxi's monitor: "NPR News: President Hernandez." The audio stream came on: "Vice President Cranmore described herself as 'optimistic' that the President and the First Lady would answer all questions at their press conference, later today. The Vice President said President Hernandez had assured her that the accusations were false, and that she could count on 'total, immediate and absolute transparency.' Rachel Richards did not answer our calls or respond to emails…"

I called Kate. "What the hell's going on?" I asked, as soon as she answered.

"What have you heard?"

"NPR said you were denying wrongdoing about something having to do with Rachel. And if I speak Washingtonian – and I do – Cranmore is fucking pissed off. That's all I know. What happened?!"

"The pigs, Marco."

"The pigs?"

"Rachel had, um, contact with the 'Animals R Us' people, before they set them loose."

"Oh, Jesus!" I thought back to how much Rachel had known about the pigs. "The media's going to go crazy! What kind of contact?"

"Well, it seems one of the young men, I mean…she was… she's…"

"Please, don't say it, Kate. Please don't say it!"

"She's pregnant, and the father is…"

"Shit!" I interrupted her: "Did she have anything to do with it? The pigs, I mean?"

I turned on the video. Tears streamed down Kate's cheeks. "You're in a car," she observed.

"On my way to the airport. I'm going to Italy."

"Ah, che bello! Non l'avrei mai pensato! I never imagined it would come to this!"

I continued in English: "So, did she? Did she have anything to do with, you know, the pigs?"

Kate hesitated before saying it: "None of us are saints, Marco! None of us are saints!"

I remembered furtive glances and knowing looks between her and Rachel.

"How much did YOU know?"

Her silence was deafening.

"Listen, Kate. I can help you only if you tell me everything."

But as I looked out the rear window at the monuments of Washington, D.C. fading into the distance, I realized I couldn't help her, no matter what she said. The truth was the truth.

"Kate, belay that request. If you and Rachel are telling the truth…"

"It isn't simple…"

"It never is, dear friend. It never is."

The screen went blank and the audio news report came back on: "The House Re-publican leadership released a statement saying that it was their oversight responsibil-ity…"

"Monitor off!" I shouted.

The cab pulled into the airport. I looked to the sky. A plane rose and turned toward the Atlantic.

***

The shop was on a cobblestone side street in the old center of Cremona. I looked into the window at the violins for sale, and others on a long table, in various stages of as-sembly or disassembly. The door was open, so I stepped inside and placed my small leather suitcase on the floor. A bell announced me. I smelled wood and glue.

"C'e' nessuno?" I called out. "Anyone here?"

"Arrivo subito! I'll be right there!" The voice came from the back of the shop, fol-lowed by a man about ten years older than I. I asked if he was Enzo.

He looked at me and smiled: "Marco?"

I nodded, wondering if Mary had called to announce that I was on my way.

"I recognized you from the news reports," he said in Italian. Guess she hadn't called him.

"What a joy to see you! When I read that you had quit your job with the Presi-dent…" he placed his hands on my shoulders. "…Maria will be so happy!"

We hugged each other as brothers do.

***

Enzo called Maria and arranged to meet at the house they still shared. He gestured toward the shop door, locked it, and took my arm. Walking toward the piazza, he greeted several people, all of whom regarded me with curiosity. He introduced me only as "an old friend."

"I don't mind if you tell people who I am," I said.

He shook his head: "We should be discreet." I furrowed my brow. "I'll explain when Maria arrives."

Even in his dusty work clothes, Enzo was distinguished-looking, with salt-and-pepper curls, the athletic physique of a younger man, and an enchanting smile. He spoke rapidly with a northern accent, explaining to me that neither he nor Maria had ever married or had children, and that they still lived together in the house that had belonged to our grandparents.

"Neither of you married?" I asked.

He smiled and didn't respond. I had the sensation that it was the wrong question.

"We always hoped you would find us someday. When we discovered recently where you were, we asked for permission to contact you."

"Permission?"

"We will explain," he said. "Maria will meet us at home."

As we walked across the expansive Piazza Stradivari, I looked up at a medieval tower.

"Il Torrazzo di Cremona — the tallest campanile in Italy!" he said proudly. "And the most beautiful."

We ascended the front stoop of their home. As he inserted the key into the old wooden door, I heard my name. I turned back toward the street as a handsome older woman in medical scrubs and white sneakers ran to me. "Marco! Is it really you?" she said in Italian, tears in her eyes. She had the same salt-and-pepper curls as Enzo. I dropped my suitcase and we kissed each other twice on the cheeks and embraced.

Maria stepped back to look at me, her hands on my shoulders, commenting that I looked like our father. Passing neighbors smiled and waved as they walked by. Enzo opened the door and carried my suitcase inside. Maria gently pushed me into their modest but attractive living room. She walked immediately to the mantle and took down two picture frames. She handed me one and smiled. It was of me as a toddler, standing by the Stradivari statue. Then she placed the other picture in my hands. It was a photo of her, perhaps nine years old, and Enzo, about eleven. Behind them were our grandparents with me on my grandfather's knee. He was drinking a glass of red wine.

"Our mother took this photo..." *Maria said*, "...about 40 years ago. It was the last time we saw her in person."

I tilted my head.

"They said it was for everyone's safety."

***

Maria showed me around the house that had been our grandparents'. It was well-kept and elegant, in the unpretentious way I would have expected from children of my own mother. A French door opened onto a balcony. We stepped outside and looked over the piazza, toward the bell tower. The smell of onions frying in olive oil mingled with voices and the sound of footsteps below.

She took me to the kitchen and sat me down at a small table. Enzo pulled a bottle of spumante rosato *from a small refrigerator and worked the cork, as Maria prepared a plate of olives, local cheeses and fresh bread. After placing it on the table in front of me, she ruffled my hair and grinned:* "Marcolino!" *she exclaimed.*

Enzo popped the cork and filled three flutes.

"To our long-lost little brother!" *Maria beamed.* "How we missed him all these years!" *Enzo added.*

"And to my family in Cremona!" *I smiled, as I raised my glass.* "I'm so happy to be here with you!"

Maria stood next to me as Enzo began chopping onions and mortadella. "We usually make fresh pasta on Sundays," *she explained*, "but this is a special occasion. Do you know 'marrubini cremonesi?'" *she asked.* "It's a local specialty. Like* agnolotti."

I nodded.

She moved to the end of the table, next to Enzo, and dusted some flour on the counter. I watched my siblings, cooking together and wondered a bit less why they had both chosen to remain single. I asked if there was anything I could do to help. Maria, her hands buried in pasta dough, pointed with her head toward an old photo album on top of an oak cabinet. I grabbed it and placed it on the table.

"I am so glad I was able to track you down here in Cremona!" I said.

They responded with perplexed looks. "It's complicated," I said. "Let me explain..."

"No. Let us explain," Maria interrupted. "You must be wondering many things. We should start from the beginning. Did Mamma ever tell you why she took only you to America? Why she left us here?"

I shook my head. "I didn't even know you existed. She said she had fled our father. That he was an abusive alcoholic."

They looked at each other.

"We understand," Enzo said. "She was forbidden to tell you about us, but now we will tell you everything,"

"But first you must know that Mamma did nothing wrong," Maria added. "She had no choice but to take you and leave us here."

"No choice?"

"She also said some things to protect you. Things that were not entirely true," Enzo looked deep into my eyes as he spoke.

"Protect me from what?"

He didn't answer my question. "After they told us she had died, we asked for permission to go find you. But they refused."

"Permission? Whose permission?"

Enzo chopped onions as he spoke, hammering the wooden board harder than was strictly necessary. "Our mother didn't exactly decide to move to America. She had a good life here in Cremona, with our father – who was NOT an alcoholic! – and our grandparents. We all lived in this house – it was a little tight, with three generations, but she was happy. Nonna and Nonno loved taking care of us, and this enabled her to do her work, to which she was so dedicated."

When I was growing up in Washington, Ma had a boring job, pushing paper around at the Italian Embassy – she was glad to have it, but I never thought it was anything more than a job. "What was so great about her work? What did she do?"

Enzo and Maria looked at each other before looking back at me. "Well, she pretended to work with our father at the luthier shop," Enzo said.

"Pretended?" I noticed that Maria had finished her spumante. I picked up the bottle to refill her glass, but she waved her hand to indicate one was enough.

Enzo continued: "It wasn't really what they did. The shop was a front. In reality, they were undercover police."

I placed my empty wine glass on the table. "Our parents were...cops?"

"Undercover. No one knew about their work, not even our grandparents, until..."

Maria interrupted him: "We were just kids, so we knew nothing. But our parents had infiltrated a terrorist cell that was preparing a bombing. The decision was made in Rome to break up the cell before they could do it. But the raid blew our parents' cover..."

Maria stopped speaking, her eyes moist. Enzo picked up where she had left off:

"A week later, they gunned our father down on his way to work. I was eleven and Maria was nine. You were a baby..."

I winced.

In the silence that followed, I wondered why so many years passed between Maria's birth and mine. She must have read my mind: "I suppose you must have been an accident," she smiled, before continuing where Enzo had left off:

"So, to keep us safe, they announced that BOTH our parents had been killed. They had a public 'funeral,' with our grandparents and the two of us present. By then, Mamma and you were on your way to Washington." She tilted her head at the photo book. I opened it. It contained several more photos of us together as children, as well as old newspaper articles about our heroic parents and their "funeral."

Enzo continued: "The terrorists who shot him were put into solitary confinement. But sooner or later their comrades might have figured out that our mother was still *alive. They would go looking for her. So the government gave her a new look, a new name and a low-profile job far away, in Washington. Of course, we had no idea where they had sent you..."*

"Why didn't...?"

Maria anticipated my question and answered it: "The government thought the best way to protect her – and you – was to leave her two 'orphans' here with her parents. It made her 'death' more credible, you see? If we all had disappeared, the terrorists would have known she wasn't dead, and gone looking for her."

"But you were just kids," I said. "Kids who had lost their father – and now you were losing your mother..."

Maria continued. "They had us meet with all sorts of people, psychologists and so on, to determine if we, and our grandparents, were capable of keeping the secret. They determined we could, and..."

Enzo interjected, "They kept us under close observation for years. Periodically, they would report that you and Mamma were fine, but they refused to say where you were. They promised that if we kept the secret, we would see you both again."

"That's why they let her take me here to visit when I was still too young to understand..."

Maria nodded, "...or to remember. We think it also was a test – to see if we would keep our secrets. Ma was forbidden to tell us where you lived, and we were forbidden to ask. We did everything they told us to, in the hope that eventually they would tell us where you were. But they never did."

"Fucking idiot bureaucrats!" Enzo's anger surprised me.

"Years later," Maria continued, "they came and told us she had died. We begged them to let us contact you. By then, we were all adults, our grandparents were gone, the terrorism threat was over. There was no good reason..."

"Our requests were always denied!" Enzo said, chopping the mortadella furiously. "We eventually found out you were in America, of course, when you started showing up in our web searches, and then in the news reports – but they had threatened to arrest

us and take the house away if we tried to contact you! They said Ma had signed some-thing..."

I stood up and put my hand on Enzo's shoulder. *"The important thing is that we finally found each other. It took far too long, but the family is together again," I paused, "and I guess there is no harm in telling you how I found you. Ma told one person..." I hesitated, wondering if I should mention Mary.*

"It's OK!" Maria said, raising her hand. "We don't need to know." She gestured me to help her stuff the marrubini *with the mixture of chopped mortadella and cheese that Enzo had made.*

As she showed me how to press the soft pasta into the correct shape, I realized I already knew how it was done.

***

I stayed several weeks in Cremona, losing count of how many times my sister and brother had invited me to stay. They introduced me to a few friends as "a relative from America." None were so indelicate as to ask too many questions.

One sunny morning, I was sitting at a café on the piazza Stradivari, drinking a cappuccino and reading the Washington Post. *The news was bleak. The Republicans were all 'Pig-gate scandal' all the time. So far, Vice President Cranmore was holding her fire and avoiding the media, but how long would that last?*

"Ciao, Marcolino!" Maria, dressed casually in jeans and a floral blouse, beamed at me as she sat down.

"Ciao." I smiled back and hugged her.

"Little one!" Enzo sat down next to her.

I looked up at the Torrazzo, before turning back to them and saying it: "I need to leave, at least for a while."

There was sadness in Maria's eyes. "We understand. But we know you will return."

"Your room will always be there for you," Enzo added. "Please come back, soon. Maybe to stay?"

"I'll come back," I said. "I promise. But I have things to take care of in America. The President is in difficulty. And, they are my friends – I need to help them. If I can."

***

It was raining in Milan when Enzo and Maria saw me off at Malpensa airport. They stepped out of the taxi with me. Enzo grabbed my bag, but I urged them to leave me on the curb, so that our tears could hide behind the raindrops. We waved until they were out of sight.

I don't recall checking in or waiting at the gate – my head was exploding with memories, reflections, dreams, hopes – and schemes for how I might help Hernandez survive the crisis threatening his presidency. As I settled into my seat, and looked out the window at the baggage ramp, I saw my own suitcase climb and then disappear into the plane's belly. I wondered how it was possible that my brother and sister, who had not seen me since I was a toddler, could have so easily and instinctively loved me. I thought of Alexandra and Rachel.

The plane flew north over the Alps. From my window, I admired the expanse of white peaks, until the mountains turned to green hills and then the fields and forests and villages of France. I picked up my Reader. One article was about pigs tearing up a little league field and a cemetery in Minneapolis. Another reported that herbicide-resistant switchgrass had shown up on opposite ends of the Eurasian Steppe. There was the usual, yearly appeal by the UN Secretary General for an end to real meat, nuclear weapons, and fossil fuels.

I looked at the jet engine outside my window, spewing its slow death, and then back to my Reader. President Hernandez, the article reported, was still maintaining that he knew nothing about the pigs and would speak to the nation once more that evening about "Pig-gate." The First Lady and both of her daughters apparently were all bedridden with an influenza they had given each other.

I wondered who might be coaching Dick and preparing his remarks. The least I could do would be to look them over. I wondered if there was anything he might say that could convince the nation of his innocence. As the blue of the Atlantic passed below on this incredibly clear day, I thought of how we might turn this resignation-worthy scandal into a speedbump, as Reagan had with Iran-Contra, Clinton had with Lewinski, and Trump had with, well, take your pick.

I pulled up Kate's number. Suddenly, a Flash notice appeared on the screen. I opened it – a subpoena from the Senate Oversight Committee, big surprise. I decided to call Dick first. "Potus Secure Line" appeared on the menu. My finger hovered over the screen. I looked out the window again at the engine spewing out toxic fumes.

I put the phone back into my pocket and watched whitecaps breaking far below me. Thousands of them. Millions. Each whitecap looked tiny from my altitude, but up close each would be terrifyingly huge. Powerful enough to capsize boats and crush the limbs of sailors, and yet existing but for seconds. Seconds of power before the inevitable collapse into the wave that bore it, and into the ocean that bore the wave. Only to be replaced by another whitecap doomed to meet the same fate. Every day, billions of them around the world, rising and then falling back into the ocean's embrace.

I wondered about the lies that had poisoned so much of my life. The lies that others had told me, and the lies that I had told others. Above all the lies that I had told myself. I considered how reality somehow eventually catches up with the falsehoods.

I took out my phone again. It rang once and I hung up. I took a deep breath, dialed again, and listened. With each ring I felt a bit freer – like a whitecap experiencing its brief moment of power before its welcome collapse.

The call went to voice mail. As the message played, I thought of what I might say, of what I must not say. But after I heard the beep, I spoke naturally, knowing that I didn't have to say anything other than the facts.

"Hi Mary," I said. "It's Marco. It's been a long, strange trip, but I'm on my way home."

THE END

Acknowledgements

I wish to thank the following authors and writers for their invaluable critiques, insights and advice: Bernard Sterchi, Letizia Osti, Anthony Haywood, Anthony Tenczar, Susan Kushner Resnick, Peter Krumpe, Lisa Durham, Randee Falk, Sari Wilson.

Special thanks to Fernanda Calvo Gómez for the wonderful cover she designed, and to my scientist wife, Leena Contarino, for patiently explaining to me all about genetically modified organisms, telomeres, mitochondria, vectors, zygotes and all that other science stuff, so that I could come to the conclusion that it would be wise not to burden my readers with any of it.

Many thanks also to Dave Gold, Paul Begala, Bill Richardson, Richard Bank, Linda Marquette, Charlie Berman, Brian Franklin, Betty Gluck, and to Carla, Lisa and Dave Contarino for their encouragement, kind words, and good counsel.

Finally, thanks to the many people I have encountered inside the mutually orbiting bizarro worlds of campaign politics, academia, and journalism, who inspired this work of satirical fiction.

About the Author

Michael Contarino received his Ph.D. in Political Science from Harvard University and he has taught at several universities in Italy, Switzerland, Britain and the US. He also served as a UN Economic Affairs Officer and as a senior policy advisor and speechwriter to a US Presidential candidate. Now Professor Emeritus at the University of New Hampshire, he lives in Switzerland with his Finnish wife, Leena, his American dog, Kofi, and his Vulcan cat, Mr. Parker. When not cycling, hiking, skiing, or arguing with his friends about whether it is ever acceptable to put cheese on shellfish, he writes political satire.

Other Books by Michael Contarino

My Father's Century

Phake News

A Political Problem

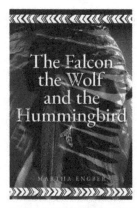

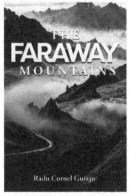